Praise for Nikki Carter

"Gia makes me want to holler out loud—
for herself and she definitely has enough
pages! I soooo loved Gia's voice. She's r
will love her, too!
—Michelle Stimpson, author of T

"Gia Stokes might be a Hi-Stepper, but this teen role model has
both feet on the ground as she meets life's challenges with style
and grace."
—Melody Carlson, author of the Diary of a Teenage Girl series

"*Step to This* is hot, it's new, it's now . . . with characters that leap
from the pages, it's absolutely a must-read."
—Monica McKayhan, *Essence* bestselling author of *Indigo Summer*

"*Step to This* is a wonderful, witty tale that is full of
laugh-out-loud moments and great lessons."
—Victoria Christopher Murray, author of The Divas series

"Nikki Carter is a fresh, new voice in teen fiction! *Step to This* has it
all—drama, humor, and a lesson that everyone can learn from. Full
of fun-loving, unforgettable characters that readers will love, Nikki
has written a page-turner that will leave the reader wanting more!"
—ReShonda Tate Billingsley, author of The Good Girlz series

"*Step to This* has alluring characters, wonderful scenes, and a
fascinating premise. Nikki Carter has a real talent for writing stories
that deal with real issues, but are gripping to read by teens and
adults alike."
—Jacquelin Thomas, author of the Divine series

"Filled with smart and witty characters, *Step to This* is a fun,
fast-paced read teens will love."
—Ni-Ni Simone, author of *A Girl Like Me*

"Nikki Carter steps up and delivers a home run with her debut
novel, *Step to This*. It's a real winner."
—Chandra Sparks Taylor, author of *Spin It Like That* and *The Pledge*

Also by Nikki Carter

Step to This
It Is What It Is
It's All Good

Published by Kensington Publishing Corporation

cool like that

A So For Real Novel

nikki carter

KENSINGTON PUBLISHING CORP.

www.kensingtonbooks.com

To my nieces Kenisha and Sierra

Acknowledgments

I always thank God first, because it's because of Him that I have the ability, tenacity, and opportunity to write. This is the dream I've always wanted!

Thank you, family, for missing days at the pool and real dinners while I finished this manuscript. I appreciate and love you (even when I'm fussing)! Brent, my love, thank you for not complaining too much when I hog the laptop.

Thank you to all my friends who encourage me daily! Afrika, Tiffany T., Myesha, Shawana, Kym, Brandi, Leslie and J-Vizzle, Krystal, and Andre: Hollerations!

I'd like to thank the staff at Kensington—Mercedes, Adeola, and Mickie: You rock! Mercedes, thank you for extensions and for Happy Monday e-mails.

To all the educators like Ms. Carol Missry, in Wall, New Jersey—thank you for sharing my books with your students! Last but not least, I'd like to thank a few of my young readers: Quinn, Brandice, Kahjanee, Ayana, Kaneesha, and Lady J! Thank you for enjoying my books!

—Nikki

cool like that

"**M**om, come on! Mrs. Freeman is going to be here in a minute."

I seriously think that my mother, Gwen, is trying to make me miss my flight. Where am I going, you ask? To a summer enrichment program in New York City! How hot is that?

What's even hotter is that my bestie, Ricky Freeman, is going too. We get to stay on a college campus all summer long, taking classes and kicking it all over the Big Apple. Man, that's hot to the touch, okay!

My mom has been tripping since she found out Ricky is going to the program instead of my other bestie, Kevin Witherspoon. Kevin got selected first, but his grandparents are really old-fashioned, and they wouldn't let him go away for the entire summer. That's how Ricky got a chance to roll.

I know what you're thinking. Why would my mom have a problem with Ricky if he's my bestie?

Well, the problem is not with Ricky per se. She's known him since he was a baby, and we've been best friends since elementary school. We even go to the same church.

The issue is with the fact that it seems like, overnight, Ricky got superduper fine. He's tall, with caramel-colored skin and big brown eyes, he keeps a low fade, his acne's disappeared, and he's got muscles he's never had before. And check it: all that extra fineness is crushing on little ol' me.

My mom wants the truth, but she can't handle the truth.

She's been asking me questions ever since our debutante ball this past spring. Ricky was my escort, and I think that made her even more paranoid.

The killer part is we aren't even dating. Not openly or secretly. Ricky suggested that we put our crushes on hold while we go to New York so my mom could trust us.

In theory, it sounds like a good plan: Gia and Ricky, buddy-buddy, without a crush in sight. In reality it might be somewhat hard to execute, especially with all the alone time we're gonna have.

Honestly, I think my mom didn't want to let me go, but she couldn't give me a good reason why I shouldn't be allowed to, after she'd already given me permission. She tries to be fair most of the time. Sometimes she comes up short, but mostly she's good.

The only thing that kicks rocks about this summer is the fact that my cousin and other bestie, Hope, won't be in New York either. I've promised to keep her updated by text, e-mail, and Facebook. With all our technology, she shouldn't miss one second of all the action.

"Gia, do you have extra underwear?" my mom asks.

She's standing in the center of the living room, looking frazzled as I don't know what. My mom is hereby prescribed a bottle of chill juice, for real.

"Mom, I've probably got enough underwear in my suitcase that I won't have to do laundry once the entire summer."

"What about your cell phone? Do you have your charger?"

"Phone, check. Charger, check."

My mother sighs. "Okay, make sure you call me before your plane takes off. Then call me when you land. After that, call me in the morning, once during the day, and before you go to bed."

She gets the *are you kidding me* blank stare.

My younger sister, Candy, says, "Dang, Mama Gwen. When is she supposed to have any fun if she's doing all that calling?"

"This trip is not about fun, it's about getting her into a good school," my mother explains. "You've got money, right? And an ATM card?"

She knows I have everything because we did a check, double-check, and triple-check yesterday. And the day before that.

She's tripping.

Finally, I hear Mrs. Freeman's horn blaring outside.

"Mom, Ricky and his mom are here! I've got everything on the list, and if I forget something, you can mail it to me."

"Okay, Gia, give me a hug."

I give hugs to my mom, sister, and my stepdad, LeRon. They are quick hugs because we've already wasted enough time, and I don't want to be late for my flight.

My mom and LeRon follow me outside to the car. I knew they were going to do that, so I try not to get irritated, but I'm not sure if it's working.

"Hey, Gia!" Ricky says as he puts my suitcase in the trunk. "Are you kidding me? What do you have in here?"

"Clothes, shoes, hair products. The usual."

Ricky shakes his head. "It feels like you have ten sets of encyclopedias in there."

LeRon clears his throat. "Ricky and Gia, we've got some ground rules for you all while you're away for the summer."

Ground rules? I can already tell this is going to steal my joy.

"Number one, remember that you belong to God and that He can see everything you're doing all the way in New York."

Wow! He put the "God sees all" rule on us. If I was planning to hook up with Ricky or any other hot boy, that just totally killed it.

"Number two, have fun!" my mom says. "We trust you and know that you'll make us proud."

"That's all?" I ask.

Gwen cocks her head to one side. "I can come up with some more if you want."

My mom hugs me and Ricky one last time before we get in the car and finally pull off. Ricky's mother looks at us in the rearview mirror and smiles.

"I've got my own rule," she says. "Please go up there and act like you've got some home training."

That means for us not to do anything stupid that would end up embarrassing our families. That's a given.

I glance over at Ricky sitting next to me in the backseat. He's wearing the Tennessee Titans jersey I gave him for Christmas last year. Cute. I'm wearing his gifts too: a charm bracelet and a butterfly barrette.

Yeah, Ricky went totally overboard last year with his gifting. He told me he was giving me the barrette because I reminded him of a butterfly. How is it that it seemed so much less corny the first time I heard it on Christmas Day?

I close my eyes and inhale deeply. Ricky's wearing some kind of cologne that smells really nice. Or maybe that's drier sheets and laundry detergent. All I know is he's smelling fresh and clean.

It's going to take all my strength and the prayers of all the ladies in the church for me to resist the power of the crush. I really want to fight it, but without distractions from people at home, this could be the opportunity Ricky and I need to finally make it official.

And, of course, we've got to be official by senior year. Hello!

I feel the excitement building in my stomach as we pull up to the airport terminal. There is a flight attendant waiting on us at the door because we're flying as unaccompanied minors. It almost feels like a babyish kind of thing, but when I found out that my mom wouldn't let me fly without the extra supervision, I gave up my issues with it.

With our escort (babysitter), we get to go through the security checkpoint without standing in line. Sweet!

Finally, we're seated in the gate area until takeoff time, which is about thirty minutes from now. I'm about to plug in my iPod and listen to some Sasha Fierce when Ricky taps me on the shoulder.

"What's up, Ricky Ricardo?"

His eyes are wide and excited. "We're going to New York City. For the entire summer. No parents."

"I know, right!"

"Gia, this is going to be the best summer of our lives. We're about to make it hot."

I can't do anything but nod in agreement. Hotness indeed. Hotness to infinity!

★ 2 ★

Okay, so why is my New York City adventure getting off to a bad start already? You would think that Ricky and I would be sitting next to each other on the plane, but no. I'm two rows behind the first-class seats, and Ricky's close to the back. There's no telling who I'm going to have to sit next to now!

Lord, please don't let it be someone smelly or extra large.

I play with my shiny cornrows and the butterfly barrette that's clipped into the side. Looking out the window is making me even more anxious to take off. I open a little compact mirror that's in my purse and refresh my strawberry mint lip gloss to take up the time. Then flip through the *SkyMall* magazine they stuff in the back of airline seats. Umm . . . do people really buy massage beds for their dogs? And if so, why would they be thinking of said purchase while they're on an airplane?

After putting the magazine back in its place, I lean my

head back and close my eyes. Maybe if I take a nap, this time will fly by.

"Hello. I think you're in my seat."

So much for my nap. But for real, for real, if my nap just had to be cut short, at least I'm waking up to a cutie.

The boy standing in front of me has to be near my age. He's cocoa brown, and not the ashy kinda cocoa—the smooth, make-you-wanna-reach-out-and-touch-it cocoa. Nice.

"Umm . . . let me see. My seat is nine-C. Is that what yours says too?"

He brushes the long, shiny locs out of his face. "Yes. Mine says nine-C too. Great."

With an annoyed look on his face, he signals for the flight attendant. "Do you mind if I sit here?" he asks me as he motions to the empty seat next to me while he waits for the attendant.

"I don't mind at all. Help yourself."

"Thank you. I'm Rashad, by the way. What's your name, Princess?"

The smile is involuntary. Dang, I'm cheesing extra hard. My brain is trying to tell my teeth to separate so I can answer the question, but they aren't listening!

"Gia," I force myself to reply. "My name is Gia."

Rashad smiles back. "Gia. That fits you. It means 'flower in bloom.' "

"It does?"

"I just made that up, I'm afraid," he says with a mischievous smile. "Are you mad?"

Memo to my brain: *Stop with the grinning already!*

He's gonna think I'm mentally challenged. "No, I'm not mad."

The flight attendant stops in front of our row. "What can I help you with, young man?"

"This young lady and I are assigned to the same seat," Rashad says.

He hands the flight attendant both of our plane tickets. She squints and reads the tickets with a perplexed look on her face.

"This is odd. Just hang out here until I come back, mmmkay?"

Rashad nods. "Okay. No problem."

"I hope they didn't make a mistake and overbook this flight," I say, "because I cannot wait to get to New York, and it would totally suck lemons if you had to go on the next flight."

"That is the truth, Princess. For real. Are you going on vacation? You with your family?"

"No, I'm . . . Wait a minute, how do I know you're not some criminal trying to scam me? I don't play that."

A huge grin bursts across Rashad's face. Ooo! Please, God, don't let him be a criminal! He's way too cute for felonious activities.

"That's funny, but I am not a criminal. I'm going to New York to a summer program at Columbia University."

Thank you, thank you, thank you!

"Word? Me too. What a coincidence."

"I know, right? What are the odds that I have a seat mix-up with another person from the program? Do you think it means anything?"

I bite my lip to keep from foolishly grinning again. "What do you think it means?"

"Maybe that we're supposed to be friends. That would be cool, right?"

"It would be totally cool." What is *wrong* with me? Did I forget that my longtime crush and best friend forever is sitting on this plane with me? I'm getting my serious flirt on like Ricky doesn't even exist. What is up with that?

Thank goodness the flight attendant comes back. She says to Rashad, "Yes, there has been a mix-up on the tickets. I apologize for that. But, fortunately, the seat you're in is not assigned. You don't mind an aisle seat, do you?"

"No, I don't mind. I'm just glad I'm getting to go. I didn't want to get stuck flying standby."

"You're all set then. We'll be taking off soon, so go ahead and get comfortable."

The flight attendant walks off with an armful of blankets and pillows to a mother and her two crying babies. I sure hope they fall asleep soon or that somebody finds a piece of candy to pop in their mouths.

"This is your first year going to the summer program, right? I would've remembered you if you'd been before."

I nod. "This is my first year, and my friend Ricky's too."

"Your friend. Is he on the flight?"

"Yes, he's somewhere back there." I point to the back of the plane.

Rashad glances over his shoulder. "Do you want to sit next to him? I can switch seats with him if you want."

"N—no. That's okay. You don't have to do that," I say.

Did I just sound really thirsty or what? Womp, womp on me.

"Okay, then, I'll stay. What classes are you taking in the program?" Rashad asks.

"Oh, I'm doing the creative-writing curriculum. I'm going to be a writer."

"Me too. Sweet."

"Where are you from, Rashad? I hear an accent, but I can't place it."

"You can hear my accent? I've been trying to hide it. I'm from Atlanta."

"Ah, that's it. You sound like my down-South cousins."

Rashad smiles. "And you sound like my up-North aunties."

"I might be going to college in Atlanta. Spelman is on my list of schools."

Rashad's eyes light up. "Word? I'm hoping to hear back from Morehouse myself. We'll be neighbors."

"That would be hot."

"Gia, we are going to have a great time this summer."

"We are?"

Rashad touches my arm, and I nearly jump out of my seat. His touch is electric.

"Yes. Have you ever been to New York?"

I shake my head. "No. I went online and found some cool places I want to visit."

"The best places aren't online."

"Then how am I supposed to find them?" I ask.

"You were supposed to meet me on this flight so I could show them to you."

I let out a half laugh, half snort. "Seriously? Wow, you've got it all figured out, I see."

"Glad to provide some humor, Princess."

"Why do you keep calling me that?" I ask.

"What? Princess?"

"Yeah."

He lifts an eyebrow. "You don't like it?"

"It just seems a little . . . I don't know . . . like maybe we should get to know each other first before you start giving me nicknames."

"I call every young lady I meet a princess."

I feel really stupid right now. I thought he was giving me a pet name or something.

"So is your friend Ricky really your boyfriend, and you're just saying he's your friend to throw your mother off the trail?"

"Uh . . . not exactly. Not officially."

Rashad chuckles. "So does that mean I still have a shot?"

"A shot at what?"

"Being your summer crush?"

"Anything's possible I suppose."

★ 3 ★

I'm completely stoked when the plane lands. New York City! I'm here!

Rashad stays close by when we get off the plane, which causes some inappropriate mean mugging by Ricky. But I think Rashad can sense that because he sticks out his hand right away for Ricky to shake.

After hesitating for a second too long, Ricky does shake his hand. "I'm Ricky Freeman. You are?"

"Rashad Moore. I met Gia on the plane. I had the pleasure of sitting next to her."

Totally blushing right now. Ricky is giving me a blank stare too, like he's trying to figure out what's going on in my head. If I knew what was going on in my head, I would definitely let him know.

I spent the entire flight getting to know Rashad, and he's cool as what. And fine as all get out. And we're in the same program too? What the heck kinda coincidence is that? Especially since Ricky is in the engineering program and will be crunching numbers all summer.

Is it possible to have more than one crush at a time? I know I can have celebrity crushes and real-boy crushes and it's okay, but two real-boy crushes? I don't know the rules on that.

"Are you in the Columbia program too?" Ricky asks.

"Yep. This is my third year," Rashad replies.

Why is Ricky looking like he wants to square up and chop Rashad down with a two-piece? Unnecessary roughness for real. Ricky and his big ego can go somewhere else. The funniest part though is that Rashad seems completely oblivious to Ricky's macho-man routine. Ha!

"I guess we should go over to the baggage claim," Rashad says.

Ricky replies, "Yeah, yeah. I knew that."

Okay, Ricky is totally tripping with these caveman shenanigans. Rashad hasn't done anything threatening yet. We've just spent a couple hours chatting. No harm there.

The baggage-claim area at this airport is a complete zoo. I'm used to the airport in Cleveland—that's pretty tame compared to this. Ricky looks a little confused too, so Rashad leads the way.

"It might take a while for our luggage to unload," Rashad says. "Depending on the airline, it can be kinda slow."

"You travel a lot?" I ask.

"Yeah. My dad is the head lawyer for an export company that does a lot of trade overseas. I've been to Europe, China, and most recently Dubai. But we come to New York more than anything."

"Sounds exciting," I say. "I've never been out of the country, unless Canada counts. I've been to Niagara Falls on a church bus trip."

"Canada is another country," Ricky says.

Rashad smiles at me and brushes my long cornrows back. "Technically, you're international, Princess."

Ricky rolls his eyes and frowns. And with good reason now. Rashad is seriously moving in on his territory, and he's bold with it too. His swagger is sick!

"Here come the bags!" I say. I'm totally happy for the diversion.

Thank God, our suitcases come up quickly. I had a little bit of anxiety about my luggage getting lost. That was a direct result of my mom's brainwashing. Gwen made me put a whole set of clothes in my carry-on bag in case my suitcase disappeared and I had to wait days to get my stuff.

Ricky grabs my bag off the belt. "Gia, here's your bag. You are straight tripping with the amount of stuff you have in here."

"A princess has got to look the part, right?" Rashad asks.

I'm dead, y'all. I just rolled over on the floor and died! Rashad is really trying to start some drama.

Ricky gives Rashad some tight-lipped side eye. Jesus, be a *let's all just get along* fence around me. And Ricky.

There's a man holding up a sign that says "Columbia Summer Program." He must be our ride.

"I think that guy over there is waiting for us," I say.

"He is," Rashad says. "They try to time the shuttles so they get a van full of us every time."

We make our way over to the van driver, and he shows

us to a long white van that's already full of kids. I feel my stomach jump a little. It's starting! My summer of fun is starting right now!

When we get on the van, everyone cheers. I'm guessing it's for Rashad, because they don't know me and Ricky yet. I mean, once they *do* get to know me, there will be cheering when I step up in the place. Okay, maybe not, but whateva to you and your hateration.

A very pretty, thick brown girl with a head full of curls looks Ricky up and down. "You're new. And a cutie. I'm Sienna."

I look at Ricky with my lips totally twisted. I want to see how he responds to this because this is going to determine the course of the summer, for real.

He grins extra hard and says, "I'm Ricky Freeman. Thanks, you're cute too."

YOU'RE CUTE TOO!!!!!!

Let me take a deep inhale and exhale before I explode on this boy. I know he feels pressed and all about Rashad, but this is full-fledged flirting. While Rashad was openly flirting with me, I totally danced around any real flirtations myself. Ricky is trying to catch a beat-down.

Sienna says, "Too bad for you, I have a boyfriend who lives in New York, so you'll just have to gaze upon this cuteness, wishing you were my boo."

Ricky laughs. "I guess I'll just have to live with that."

Sienna giggles and turns her attention to me. "What's your name? Love your braids. Is that your real hair?"

I force myself to reply, "I'm Gia. Yeah, it's my real hair."

"That's hot."

I feel my icy glare melt away. Sienna is truly friendly, and of course she has no idea about the history I have with Ricky.

Sienna leans up over her row in the van and gives Rashad a hug around his neck. "What's up, Rashad! It's gonna be crazy when we go to college and don't get to see each other in the summers anymore."

"I know, right! That's why we have to have a blast this year," Rashad says. "I don't know if I'm coming next summer. Might try to do some stuff at home with my friends and enjoy the end of my senior year."

"I'll be here next summer because my boyfriend lives in New York! I'll probably go to college here too," Sienna says.

After a few more kids pile into the van, we pull away from the airport. Finally, I get to see New York, even if it is through the windows of the van.

"So are you still gonna do spoken-word stuff this summer, Rashad?" Sienna asks.

Rashad replies, "If I get the opportunity. There are a few new spots I want to check out over in Harlem. My boy Leo hipped me to them."

I listen to their conversation intently, trying to learn more about Rashad. One thing I've noticed off the bat is that he hasn't called Sienna a princess yet. He told me he says that to all the girls. I'm thinking not.

His confidence is off the chain though. I love how his body movements go with what he's sayng. He's so animated it looks like the beginnings of a dance routine when he really gets going.

I see Ricky checking out Rashad too, like he's scoping out his competition. But it was Ricky's idea to have this whole "crush on hold" thing going on. So he can't be mad at me if I'm enjoying some attention. Can he?

Yeah, I was extra heated when I thought Sienna was pushing up on Ricky. I think that was just some kind of instinct though. Maybe Ricky has the same kind of thing going on. I don't know.

"We're here!" Sienna squeals.

The van driver drops us off in front of a large building. He helps us unpack our bags and leaves us to fend for ourselves. Thankfully, there are a lot of kids out here, and we've got Rashad and Sienna to show us where we need to go.

"This is Lerner Hall," Rashad explains. "This is where we sign in and get our rooming assignments."

"It's also the hangout spot!" Sienna says.

Rashad nods in agreement. "Yep. There's a cool restaurant on the upstairs level that stays open late. It's where everybody goes to hang on campus."

"Off campus is another matter entirely! We can go to the artsy spots in Harlem, some jumpin' teen spots in the Bronx and Brooklyn, or the VIP joints that pop in Manhattan," Sienna says.

It sounds like Sienna really knows something about how to par-tay! I'm gonna have to limit my kicking-it time with her. Shoot, I know I'm all the way in New York, but Gwen's mess radar can cross state lines.

Yep, I am one hundred percent afraid of what my mother would do if she heard about me partying VIP style in Manhattan. Can anyone spell B-E-A-T-D-O-W-N? My mama does not play.

Ricky tries to grab my suitcase for me to take it into Lerner Hall. How sweet and cavemanly of him.

"I've got it, Ricky," I say. "Thanks for helping me, but you've got to get your own stuff. I can handle mine."

Rashad breezes past us to meet up with some other people he probably knows from the previous summers. I watch as he hugs girls and guys alike, and I feel a little jealous that I'm not already in their clique.

"Are you coming, *Princess?*" Ricky asks.

I laugh out loud. "Is somebody hating? All you had to do was let Rashad know I'm your girl."

"I'm not pressed. Dude is lame anyway, with that chick hair hanging down his back. Looking like Simba from *The Lion King.*" Ricky waves his hand to emphasize his point and starts toward the building.

Soon after we walk in, everyone gets into lines organized by their last name. Sienna stands behind me in line.

"Last name Thompson," she explains.

I nod. "I didn't know there were gonna be so many kids here. This is great."

"Yeah. Seems like there are more than the last two years, so it's really gonna be popping this year."

Sienna's cell phone rings, and she answers it on the first ring. "Hi, baby."

I hate hearing only one side of a conversation, so I look around the room at my fellow students. This is really different from home. I thought I went to a pretty multicultural school at home. At Longfellow High, we've got Black, white, Latino, and a few Asians sprinkled in. But here there are people who really look like they come from other countries. Hotties from all over the world. Nice!

It's finally my turn in line. There's a bubbly girl sitting at the table, cheesing up at me. I can't help but smile back.

"Hi! I'm Felicity Barrow. Welcome to Columbia University."

"Hi. I'm Gia Stokes."

Felicity scans her page and smiles. "Guess what, Gia?"

"Umm, I don't know. What?"

"I'm your RA."

She says this with such excitement that I'm thinking RA stands for "really awesome"!

I ask, "And RA is short for . . . ?"

"Resident adviser. It means I'm your fun ambassador for the summer, and I'll help you with any issues you might have."

"So you're like a camp counselor?"

Sienna whispers, "More like warden."

Felicity giggles. "I guess it *is* something like a camp counselor! We're going to have a great time."

She gives me a huge stack of papers and tells me I'm in dormitory A. It's a coed dorm! How cool is that? My mom will most probably have a coronary if she finds out about this, so we're just not going to tell her.

"Now, you go stand in the line at the rear to take your ID photo," Felicity explains. "When you're done with that, you'll receive your key card for your dorm."

I groan on the inside when I glance back at the photo ID line. It's super long, and I'm tired of dragging this luggage. But I'm not gonna let it get me too twisted, because why? I'm in New York City, baby!

After a really long and exaggerated sigh, I walk over to stand in line. Rashad walks up at the same time. Niiiice. "What dormitory are you in, Princess?" he asks.

"Dormitory A."

"Me too. I'm looking forward to having pillow fights with you."

I laugh out loud. "Seriously? Dude, I don't pillow fight, but I will annihilate you in some Xbox."

"You play Halo or something?" Rashad asks.

"Uh, no. Do I look like I play shoot-'em-up games? I'm a Rock Band girl."

Rashad bursts into a flurry of giggles. "Man, you are funny."

"Thank you."

It's funny watching people pose for their ID photos. One girl just tried to give that "I'm a supermodel" tight-eyed glare. Fail. Then, a boy who probably has a 4.0 GPA attempts a hardcore hip-hop-artist nod. Epic fail!

When it's my turn, I'm feeling the pressure of the photo too. As I sit on the little round stool, I hope I don't look like a nerdbomb in my picture.

Just as the photographer tells me to get ready, I look up and see Rashad smiling at me extra hard. I totally lose focus and end up not smiling but making what I'm sure is some completely goofy expression. "Can I get a do-over?" I ask the photographer.

"Sorry. It's one and done. We've got a long line."

Rashad clutches his stomach, doubles over, and laughs. "Nice pic, Gia."

I narrow my eyes and drag my suitcase over to the ID table. I wait until Rashad is about to take his picture, then blurt out, "That's why you look like Simba from *The Lion King*!"

Rashad opens his mouth in shock just as the flash goes off. Ha! That's what he gets for rumbling with the princess.

After Rashad picks his picture up from the table, he shows it to me. "Are you satisfied?" he asks. "You've got me looking foolish."

I nod. "Yep, absolutely satisfied. Mine actually turned out cute."

"Do you really think I look like Simba?"

"No."

He sighs. "Good."

"More like Mufasa."

"Hater."

"All day, every day."

We both fall out laughing and head outside, where I meet up with Ricky and Sienna. Rashad goes off with a group of his friends.

"See you later, Princess!"

"Not if I see you first!"

Ricky gives me a blank stare. "Seriously, Gia?"

"What?"

Ricky shakes his head and asks, "What dorm are y'all in?"

"Dormitory A," Sienna replies.

"Me too! Sweet!"

Sienna says, "I think they pretty much try to group us by age, which is cool because we do not want a lot of freshmen up in our bidness."

Ricky and I pull out our handy-dandy campus maps from the registration packets. Sienna laughs.

"Put them things away!" she says. "Follow me."

"The itinerary says there's a barbeque thing later," I say. "Is that usually fun?"

Sienna nods. "Yeah, it's cool. It's where you get to scope out all the hotties and pick your summer crush. Unless you already have one."

Why did she look at me when she said that? I haven't demonstrated anything to Sienna to let her know about Ricky and I, other than a little bit of mean mugging in the van. So what is she talking about?

Okay, am I over thinking this or what? Maybe it was just a simple statement, with no deeper meaning at all.

"So you're gonna go to your room and change for the barbeque?" Ricky asks.

"Yeah, but you don't have to wait for me, because I don't know how long it will take me to get dressed. I'll meet you there."

Ricky looks stunned by my response. It doesn't have anything to do with Rashad, although I know he thinks it does. I want to meet my roommate and take my time getting dressed.

Now, if I happen to run into Rashad on my way over to the barbeque, it's all good.

What? Don't give me a blank stare. Ricky is the one who started this "no-crush summer" mess. It's all his fault.

Sienna drops me off at my suite. "I'm right upstairs in room four-oh-nine-B. You can call from room to room by dialing seven first and then the room number."

"Get the heck out of here! Like in a hotel?"

She nods. "Yep. They have maids who come in every day to clean the rooms too."

"Shut up!"

Sienna laughs and leaves me to go to her room. I open

the door to my suite with a swanky little key card. Already, I'm adding Columbia to my college list. I could get used to this.

The first thing I notice when I step into my bedroom is a strong coconut scent. It's nice—kind of earthy, but sweet, like how a day spa might smell.

"I hope you like coconut," says the girl I'm assuming is my roommate.

"I do, it smells nice. Hi, I'm Gia Stokes."

The girl walks up to me swinging her pin-straight, obviously salon-straightened tresses. Her skin is the color of butter-pecan ice cream and completely acne free (hate her). She moves like a supermodel, deliberately taking wide strides and swinging her arms as if on a runway. She stops in front of me and kisses both my cheeks. Well, she doesn't actually kiss me. She makes kissing noises in the air.

Now is the appropriate time for a blank stare.

"I'm Melody Brookstone. Something tells me we're going to be BFFs by the end of the summer."

I give her my friendliest smile. "Cool! Are you going to the barbeque?"

"Yes, even though I don't eat meat."

A real live vegetarian. Wow on top of wow.

"Is this your first summer in the program?" I ask.

"It's my second year."

"So you know a lot of people already?"

Melody nods. "Some, but I try to keep my clique intimate. More people equals more drama."

"Don't I know it," I say in agreement. "I need this summer to be drama free."

"See!" Melody exclaims. "I knew we were going to be close."

Truth be told, it is my turn not to have drama. My high school years have been drama to the infinite power. I've had a shoplifting little stepsister, frenemies, unsuccessful makeovers, boys playing me out, and friends with half-naked pictures posted on Facebook.

So seriously, can a sister get a break?

My phone buzzes in my purse. Before I even look at the caller ID, I know it's my mom.

"Hi, Mom," I say.

"Gia, why haven't you called to let me know you're safe?"

"I'm sorry. I was just about to call you. I'm in the dorm now with my new roommate, Melody."

"Mmm-hmm. Don't make me get on a plane and fly up there, Gia. You better keep in touch."

"I will, Mom. But I'm about to go to a barbeque with all the students and the resident advisers. So can I call you back?"

"Yes. Have fun, okay, and tell Ricky I said hello."

"I will."

I press "end" on my phone and open my suitcase on the little stand at the end of my bed. Melody walks over with a look of interest on her face.

"What are you going to wear?" she asks.

"I don't know. What's appropriate?"

"You should probably go with resort casual."

Resort casual? What in the world is the difference between resort casual and regular casual? I need an answer pronto. This is soooo not a rhetorical question.

Melody laughs. I guess she can tell by the befuddled expression on my face that I'm completely clueless.

She starts pulling clothes out of my suitcase. "These khaki capris and this pink baby tee. This works. Do you have any heels?"

"Heels? I have flip-flops. Is that resort casual?"

Melody's eyebrows rise almost all the way up to her hairline. "Flip-flops? Have mercy on my soul. No. You may not wear flip-flops. Please tell me you have an acceptable pair of sandals."

"I do have a few pairs." I toss the shoes into the center of the floor.

Melody taps her chin as though in deep thought. "These will do," she says as she picks up a pair of Nine West wedge heels that Hope put in my luggage. "Do you have a bag to match these?"

"I have this little pouch and a mini backpack."

"There's no time to go shopping, so I guess you'll have to borrow one of mine."

Why is it that everyone wants to give me a makeover? Why can't they just allow Gia to be Gia?

"I'll pass on the bag, Melody. My backpack works for me."

Melody looks totally wounded. "Sorry. I just wanted you to look hot for the barbeque."

"I really appreciate you for that, but I've got my own style."

Melody plops down on the bed. "Was that too much? I can pump the brakes if you want."

"It's cool, Melody. You can pick out a bag for me just this one time."

"Really?" She claps her hands together, jumps up, and hugs me.

"Umm, Gia . . . you need a shower, sweetie."

I burst out laughing. "Pretty much. I'll go handle that, and you can choose a bag while I'm in there."

I'm glad for the shower and a few moments away from my brand-new BFF. It's funny—I've never made friends with anyone this quickly, but this Melody Brookstone seems determined to have me in her clique.

After I'm fresh, clean, and dressed, I turn around in a little fashion-model pose for Melody.

"A great improvement," she says as she hands me a big leopard-skin purse.

"Leopard skin? This doesn't match anything I have on."

"Oh, you don't have to match your bag anymore, as long as it's hot."

"If you say so."

I rub my tummy, which is definitely on empty. I haven't eaten anything since the little pack of peanuts the flight attendant gave me on the plane.

"Are you ready to go now?" Melody asks.

I'm about to say yes when my phone rings. The caller ID says "Hizzle-Pizzle." Ha! That means it's my cousin Hope. And you know she was furious when she found out about her nickname in my address book.

"This will take only a sec," I say to a now-impatient-looking Melody. "Talk to me," I speak into the phone.

"Why have I not received any texts or Facebook messages yet, Gia? What's up? You are supposed to be keeping me posted."

"I'm sorry. I've been a little busy since I got here."

"Well, you need to get unbusy and tell me what's going on," Hope fusses. "Have you met anyone cool yet?"

"Yeah, my roommate, Melody, this girl named Sienna, and a cutie named Rashad."

"Rashad Moore?" Melody asks.

I nod at Melody and listen to Hope squeal. "A cutie? What's up with him? Wait a minute, what's up with Ricky?"

"Rashad is cool, but I haven't gotten a chance to know him yet. Ricky is, you know, Ricky. It's all good."

"Oooh, drama! Gia, I never pictured you being a female mack, but it's possible. Was Ricky hating on the new dude?"

"Is Tweety bald and yellow?"

I hear Hope suck her teeth. "It would be too much for you to answer a question with a simple yes or no, wouldn't it?"

"You know you like being treated to my wit."

"Whatever, Gia."

Melody clears her throat and flares her nostrils. She mouths the word *barbeque* to let me know she's ready to go.

"Okay, Hope, I've gotta go to this barbeque thing with my roommate. She's waiting for me. I'll call you later."

"You better not forget, Gia."

"All right, bye."

"It's about time," Melody says.

Melody leads the way to the patio where the barbeque is being held. The party already seems to be in full swing. Ricky's here already, and Rashad is too.

"So, you were talking about Rashad earlier. Are you crushing on him?" Melody asks.

I shrug. "Not sure yet. He seems cool though."

"Beyond cool. He's hot to death."

"Wait a minute. Are you crushing on him? Because if so, I'll step out of the way."

"Umm, no," Melody says. "I have a boyfriend back home in Boston. We're totally getting married after college."

"Really? I haven't thought much past which college I should attend, and I haven't even really decided on that either."

"Well, I've dated Wilson ever since ninth grade. I think we're soul mates."

"Wow, okay."

Is it weird for teenagers to be exclusive like that? If it is, there must be something wrong with me. I can't even decide if I want to have a crush on both Ricky and Rashad, but Melody already has her husband picked out.

"Rashad is really nice though, Gia. And cute too."

"I know, right."

Ricky waves over in my direction. "Come on, Melody," I say. "I want you to meet my best friend Ricky."

As we walk toward Ricky and his new friends, he flashes us one of his really cute smiles. I so hate myself for this, but the butterflies are flitting all over my stomach.

"He's a hottie," Melody whispers. "How is it that you can be best friends with him and not have a crush?"

"Who says I don't have a crush on him?" I respond with a giggle.

"Ooo, multiple crushes!"

"Hey, Gia!" Ricky says when we get to his group. "What took you so long?"

"You know us girls," Melody says. "We had to get beautiful. I'm Melody, Gia's roommate."

"I'm Ricky, and this is Xavier and Sushil, my roommates."

"Why are there three of y'all in a room?" I ask.

"Sushil signed up at the last second," Xavier says, "so we got stuck with a triple."

Melody gives Sushil a hug and her funny air kisses. "Hey, Shil. I didn't know you were coming back this summer. Didn't you graduate?"

"Yes, but I am attending Columbia in the fall, and my father thought it was best if I spend another summer in the program."

Sushil's accent catches me completely off guard. He looks Indian (not Native American, but from the country India), but he sounds British.

"Shil is from London," Ricky explains like he's reading my mind.

I nod. "Cool. You're coming all the way to New York for college?"

"Yes. My father went here and has a medical practice back home. One day I'm going to join him," Sushil says.

Xavier says, "I'm not coming here for college. It's too cold in the winter. I'm going to USC. What about you, Ricky?"

"I don't know. Probably a football school though. Maybe Georgia Tech because my best friend here is talking about going to Spelman."

I feel my mouth drop open a little. I didn't know he was trying to go to college near me. We've never even talked about it.

Wait a minute. Is this Ricky's sneaky little way of claiming me? I can see why he's putting that out there because Sushil is a hottie for real with his coffee-colored skin and big dark curls. Xavier, not so much. He reminds me of Kevin before his makeover.

But back to the matter at hand. Ricky claiming me? What's up with that?

Rashad walks over to us and hugs Melody. "Hey, Mel. Long time, no see."

"I know, right! How was junior year in the *A?*"

Rashad laughs out loud. "Listen at you trying to use slang. Junior year in the *A* was good, Mel."

"Hey, Gia." Rashad hugs me too. "Melody is a cool person to have for a roommate. You scored with this one."

Rashad's hug has got me feeling completely uncomfortable. One, he held me just a little bit too long, and two, Ricky is glaring at me like he wants to explode. This is not a win-win situation for me. I guess I'm not cut out to be a player.

"Hey, Rashad," I say in a nervous tone. "Is anybody hungry? I'm hungry. Oh, look, there are some hot dogs."

I can't race away from them fast enough. Melody is on my heels as I rush away.

"Are you okay, Gia? You're acting weird."

"Yep, I'm cool. Just hungry."

I grab a hot dog from the table and take a huge bite so I don't have to answer any other questions. Rashad, Ricky, Sushil, and Xavier continue talking and getting to know one another until the resident advisers get up and start going over the rules for the summer program. Midnight curfew during the week, and one in the morning on the weekends. Score! This will cause my mom to have another meltdown if she finds out. So you already know what it is—we're not telling her.

No members of the opposite sex are allowed in sleeping rooms, but we can all chill in the common areas. Of course, the advisers point out that no drugs or alcohol are allowed. They also have zero tolerance for violence.

After the cookout, everyone goes back to Lerner Hall to hang. I haven't said much of anything because I'm afraid I'll put my foot in my mouth. Ricky has been strangely quiet too.

"So who's up for a walk in Times Square?" Sushil asks.

Melody looks up from the chessboard she's setting up. "I don't know, Shil. It's late."

"We can all stay together," Rashad says. "And of course we won't stay out after curfew. It's Saturday night, so we've got until one in the morning. Gia, you have got to see Times Square at night."

I nod. "Okay. What do you think, Ricky? Do you want to come?"

"Sure. It sounds like fun. Wait—how are we going to get there?"

Sushil replies, "The subway, of course!"

We all head back to the dorm so Melody can change her shoes. She told us there was no way she was marching around Times Square in four-inch heels.

As we wait in the lobby, I ask Rashad, "Is it true what my mama says about the subway?"

He laughs. "Maybe. What does your mama say?"

Should I tell him Gwen thinks every criminal in New York City rides the subway waiting for unsuspecting teenage girls? Nah. I think not. He'll just think she's crazy. Yes, she is crazy, but he doesn't need to know that. "My mom just thinks it's dangerous."

"It can be, but we'll all be together, and we only have to ride one train to get to Times Square."

I can't read the look on Ricky's face as he stares at Rashad. I want to think that Ricky is jealous, but that wouldn't be necessary, because Rashad hasn't made any real moves.

Melody steps out of the elevator with Sienna. Oops. Why didn't I think to invite her? I had her room number and everything.

"I asked Sienna if she wanted to go too. I hope you all don't mind, but Gia and I were totally outnumbered by boys."

Sienna smiles and goes around the group getting hugs. She spends an extra amount of time with Ricky. She needs to stop tripping with that. Didn't she say she had a boyfriend anyway?

"Let's go before it gets too late," Rashad says.

We all follow Rashad's lead to the subway terminal. Gwen totally exaggerated. There is absolutely nothing scary about this so far. I'm still not one hundred percent convinced, so I'm holding my purse extra tightly. I wish I had put down Melody's giant leopard-skin monstrosity and gotten my backpack.

Rashad sits next to me on the subway car. Ricky pretends not to care and sits chatting with his roommates.

Melody and Sienna catch up on gossip about people I don't know yet.

"So is Ricky cool with us sitting hugged up like this?" Rashad whispers.

"We are not hugged up, boy. Stop playing."

Rashad leans back in his seat. "The best friends with secret crushes on one another spend their first summer alone in the big city."

"Ha-ha. You trying to write a story?"

Rashad grins. "I *am* here for the creative-writing program, Princess. That's what I do."

"Well, your story is fiction."

"I don't know, Gia, Ricky seemed to be throwing a lot of shade in my direction earlier."

"He's not throwing any now," I protest.

"That's a male-ego thing. He can't let me know he's pressed. But he is very threatened because he thinks I'm interested in you."

Dang! Why can't I wipe this stupid grin off my face? And why doesn't he stop flirting?

"Well, are you?" I ask.

"Am I what?"

"Interested?"

Rashad laughs out loud. "Why don't we just let the summer write the story. This is our stop."

Are you kidding me? *Let the summer write the story?* Wow on top of wow. This dude really is a writer because nobody talks like this in real life. I mean, for real.

We get off the train, and immediately, I see a difference. The subway station at this stop is darker, and some of the people milling around are beyond special. I feel myself step just a little closer to Rashad. Oooh, wait a minute. How is it that I didn't notice his muscular arms before? Nice!

Rashad says, "Listen, when we get to street level, everybody stay together. We don't want Ricky or Gia to get separated or lost on their first time out."

Okay, sidebar. Isn't it great how Rashad is totally taking control of the situation? I wish you could see how irritated Ricky looks. Not that I want him to be irritated, but he needs to step his game up: Rashad's swagger is eclipsing Ricky's.

Melody loops an arm through mine. "I won't lose her," she says. "Come on."

Oh, my goodness! They told me Times Square was awesome, but they so did not tell me it was like this!

Everything is lit up, there are a ton of people walking around like it's the middle of the day, and it's loud like we're at the flyest house party ever.

"This is *too* for real, Ricky!" I squeal.

Ricky shouts, "I know, right! Times Square, baby!"

I untangle myself from Melody and grab Ricky's jacket. How awesome is it that I'm sharing this experience with my best friend?

"Kevin would so love this, Ricky. Take some pictures."

"Tourist alert," Xavier says with a giggle.

Ricky and I totally ignore Xavier teasing us about looking like tourists. Whatever! We *are* tourists.

I point up the street at a brightly decorated storefront. "There's a souvenir shop! Let's stop—I want to get a T-shirt."

"First rule of shopping on the streets of NYC," Rashad says. "Never buy from the first store you see. I guarantee you'll see the same shirts up the street for cheaper."

"Whatever! This is cheap. Two for ten dollars! Let's get one each, Ricky."

Melody interjects. "Even though I wouldn't be caught dead wearing anything on that table, I'm gonna have to agree with Rashad."

I look to Ricky for his input. He shrugs. "The night is young, right? Let's keep going."

I can't keep my eyes from bouncing back and forth. Everything is so bright! I mean, seriously, there's a Jay-Z video playing on a huge video screen mounted on the side of a building. Are you kidding me?

"I'm hungry," Xavier says as we walk past a pizza parlor.

"Didn't you eat at the barbeque?" Sienna asks.

"I'm a growing boy, and my stomach is saying yes to a slice of pepperoni pizza!"

We all crack up laughing because Xavier rubs his stomach with longing in his eyes. He looks hilarious!

"You haven't had pizza until you've had it in New York," Rashad says.

Sienna rolls her eyes. "Whatever! Chicago is the spot for pizza, Rashad. You haven't had a pizza pie until you've had a five-meat, deep-dish pie from Chi-Town."

Ricky laughs. "Man, now I'm hungry!"

"We might as well stop then," Melody says.

We pile into the tiny restaurant. There are pockets of teenagers and artist types. And in the corner a couple sits sharing a slice of pizza.

Rashad scores a table for us near the window. This whole

evening so far has been cool to infinity. I feel so free, like I'm almost an adult or something. No Gwen calling to tell me to get my butt home or interrogate me about my new friends.

This is hot!

We order a large pepperoni pizza because most of us are not really hungry, and one slice should be enough for everybody except Xavier.

"So you two are from Cleveland, right?" Melody asks. "What do you all do for fun?"

"We roller-skate or go hang out at the rec," Ricky says. "Gia is on the step squad at school, so she hangs with that clique."

Sienna high-fives me across the table. "Step squad! I know that's right."

"Uh, chill with the step sisterhood. Cheerleaders rule at my school," Melody says.

"Are you a cheerleader?" Ricky asks.

"I'm not just a cheerleader, I'm the captain."

The boys burst out laughing. Ricky says through his giggles, "Cheerleading is not a real sport, Melody. You don't have to be so militant about it!"

"Hi, haters," Melody says with a neck roll.

This just makes the boys laugh harder.

The waitress brings the pizza to the table, and on first glance I don't see anything special. The crust looks super thin, definitely not like the thick pan pizzas I'm used to eating at home.

"It looks kind of flimsy to be the best pizza ever," Ricky says, mirroring my thoughts.

"Taste first, talk second," Xavier replies as he snatches a slice and bites it in one swift motion.

I take a slice for myself. The taste totally surprises me. The sauce is tangy but really good. The crust, though thin, manages to be crispy on the edges but chewy in the middle. It's delicious.

"You like?" Rashad asks.

All I can do is nod as I swallow the tasty morsels. After everyone eats a slice, we all wish we'd ordered more than one pizza.

Melody says, "Come on, y'all. We don't want to be late for curfew on our first night out."

On our way back to the Times Square subway station, we see a street vendor selling the same T-shirts I wanted to score earlier. Guess how much they're charging? Four shirts for ten dollars!

Rashad nods over at the vendor. "Gia, you want to get your shirt now?"

"Are you happy that you were right?" I ask.

Rashad rakes his hand through his locs and grins at me. "Nah. I'm not any happier because of that. But maybe you'll trust me next time."

"It's gonna take a lot more than a shopping trip to get me to trust you."

Rashad hooks his finger under my chin and laughs. "Okay, Princess."

Ricky narrows his eyes and glares at me and Rashad. At first, I was thinking that all Ricky had to do was claim me, and I'd be totally over this new crush on Rashad. But now I'm not so sure.

★ 4 ★

Later, after our Times Square adventure, Sienna hangs for a while in my room. Curfew means you only have to be off the streets and back into the building. As long as there are no boys and girls together in the same bedroom, it's all good if we stay up half the night.

Sienna sprawls across Melody's bed like she lives in our room. I vote no, but nobody asked me!

"So, Gia," Melody asks. "You and Rashad really seem to be hitting it off. I think he really likes you."

Sienna concurs. "For real. I've never seen him push up on any girl like he's on you."

"I wonder what it is. I haven't really said or done anything out of the ordinary."

"Maybe it's those cute braids," Melody says. "That barrette is really hot too. Where'd you get that?"

"Ricky gave it to me."

Sienna's eyes widen. "Go, girl! Hog all the boys! If I was as thin as you, I'd be pulling them too."

"You're kidding, right?" I ask. "I'd kill for your shape. If I had curves like you, I would never walk, I'd just pop my booty up and down the street."

I don't know why this is so funny, but we all crack up laughing.

"Speaking of this big ol' booty," Sienna says as she smacks her behind, "do you girls want to go running in the morning?"

Melody scrunches her nose. "Running where? Outside?"

"Yes, outside. If we go superearly, it'll still be cool outside, and we can go have breakfast at Sylvia's in Harlem."

"I'm down for the breakfast, but y'all can go running without me," I say. "I'm not really into athletic activities unrelated to the Hi-Stepper squad."

"Are you serious?" Sienna asks. "You don't work out on the regular? Then how do you stay so thin?"

"I wish I could gain some weight."

Sienna shakes her head sadly. "You don't know how lucky you are, Gia."

"Don't you notice how the boys look at you, Sienna?" Melody asks.

"Puh-lease. Are you going running with me, Mel?"

"Sure."

"Great. Can you boot up your laptop really quick? I need to check my e-mail, and I don't feel like going to my room yet."

Melody pulls out her expensive-looking laptop computer and hands it to Sienna. It's really fly, just like Melody, with an aqua-blue top.

"Are you checking for an e-mail from your man?" Melody asks.

"Of course!"

"She's been dating this guy since last summer," Melody explains.

"And I am so in love with him," Sienna says. "I can't believe someone like him would even want to talk to me."

"What's his name? Where did you meet?" I ask.

Sienna replies, "His name is Danny, but everyone calls him Dan Tropez."

"Why do they call him that?"

"It's his rap name. You know, like San Tropez."

"Oh . . ."

Sienna smiles as she opens her inbox. "My boo has invited us to a party tomorrow night. It's a listening party for his new album. Y'all wanna come with?"

"Sure!" Melody says. "He always has the coolest parties."

"I guess. Can Ricky come?" I ask.

"Yeah, but why would you want to bring him?" Sienna asks. "Isn't that like bringing sand to the beach?"

"You're going to be all booed up, aren't you? Are Mel and I just supposed to watch you and your man have fun?"

Melody interjects. "But if you bring Ricky, I'll be a serious fifth wheel."

"Dan can hook you up with someone," Sienna offers.

"Ew. No. Boyfriend at home. Remember?"

I ponder for a moment and then say, "Well, I guess I don't have to bring Ricky."

"Good then. Will y'all walk me up to my room? I'm tired, and I want to get up early for running."

Melody and I put on slippers and robes to cover our pajamas, and we take the elevator upstairs with Sienna to her room.

On our way back down the hall, we meet Ricky and Sushil. They both look sleepy, but they have a bucket of ice.

"What are y'all doing?" I ask.

"Xavier wants to make smoothies," Sushil says.

"At one in the morning?" Melody asks.

"Dude must have a tapeworm or something," Ricky replies, "because he says he's still hungry."

Ricky grabs my wrist and pulls me down the hall. "Hey, I wanna talk to Gia for a quick second."

Melody warns, "Don't pull her behind any closed doors. We don't want to get in trouble."

"Okay, I'll be only a minute."

Ricky stares at me while he pulls me away out of earshot of Sushil and Melody. When we've gone a far enough distance, he asks, "What's up with you, Gia?"

"Nothing. What's up with you?"

Ricky smiles and licks his bottom lip. Okay, here is the Ricky I know and crush on. It's about time he showed up in New York. I was starting to think he left him at home.

"Do I need to worry about Rashad?"

"I don't know. Do you?"

"Oh, you gonna make me work, Gia? Haven't I already put in enough work?"

I shrug. "I guess, but you're the one who said our thing was on hold this summer. Are you taking that back now?"

"Not exactly. I just don't want any other dudes pushing up on you."

"So I'm supposed to not enjoy any boy companionship this summer? Is that what you're saying?"

Ricky chuckles. "You can hang out with me, Xavier, and Sushil, but Rashad is off limits."

"What?" I snatch my hand away. "Are you trying to tell me who I can and cannot be friends with?"

"Well . . ."

"Last time I checked, you were not my father. You're not even my official boyfriend."

"But, Gia—"

"But nothing. You need to fall back with that noise, Ricky. I never took you to be a hater, but you're tripping right now. Come on, Melody. Let's be out."

Melody rushes down the hall and grabs my arm. "Good night, y'all," she says to the boys.

I'm fuming as we get on the elevator. The nerve of him! I understand him being jealous of Rashad and all. I even understand him being threatened. But for him to think he can boss me is ri-darn-diculous. I do not roll like that.

"Is everything all right?" Melody asks as soon as the elevator doors close.

"I'm cool."

"Really? Because you look the opposite of cool. You look extra heated."

I reply, "Ricky and I have been best friends since we were kids, and last year these crush feelings emerged. I don't know if we're ready for it though. He's tripping."

"Crushes have ruined the best of friendships."

"Tell me about it. He's telling me he doesn't want me around Rashad, even though our crush is supposed to be on a break for the summer."

"How do you put a crush on a break?" Melody asks.

"I don't know. I don't really want him talking to other girls either, but I wouldn't try to tell him whom he could be friends with. That's not cool."

"Yeah, that's not cool, but you gotta admit, Rashad has been laying it on thick. He's really digging you. Maybe Ricky sees that, and he's just jealous."

"True, but he needs to find a better way to communicate that."

Melody sighs. "I hope you two figure it out, because you're definitely cute together."

"Am I cute with Rashad too?"

"Yeah, unfortunately. I can't help you choose between the two, so don't ask. They're both fine."

As much as I was trying to avoid drama this summer, I'd put myself smack dab in the middle of it. And on the first day too? Drama might as well be my middle name.

★ **5** ★

After waiting for an hour, we finally get seated for breakfast at Sylvia's. From the satisfied looks of the people who are leaving, I'm about to get my grub on. My stomach just growled in agreement.

Sienna's boyfriend, Dan, showed up with a small crew of four dudes, so there are seven of us in total. I wonder if Ricky would be mad if he saw me today. Most probably, but, shoot, I'm mad at me for being seen with these thuggish-ruggish clones.

Dan actually looks pretty cool. He reminds me of that basketball player Grant Hill. He's kinda tall and thin, with a low haircut. His clothes are only kind of thuggish. But his boys . . . They look like extras from a 50 Cent film.

One of Dan's friends has been giving me the eye since he walked through the door. I'm so not in the mood to fight off his advances, but he zips his lips and says, "So, shorty, I'm digging your braids. Did you do 'em? Can you hook a brotha up?"

He definitely needs someone to hook up his braids. They look about a month old and have had fuzz and lint balls for days. I can only imagine how filthy the water will be when he finally does wash that mess. Ew.

"I don't braid. My mother did these," I reply curtly.

"Don't be mean, shorty. I'm just trying to start up a convo with you."

I force myself to smile. "It's all good. I'm just ready to get my grub on."

"Yeah, baby. You could use a few bowls of grits!"

Was that supposed to be funny? Yeah, I'm really impressed with him now. He clowns my petite frame and thinks that's flirting. I'm ready to forsake all other crushes and get with him now. *Not!*

I'm glad the waitress comes and takes our orders. Her presence interrupts the stupid conversation. And, see, I was about to order grits, but I can't now!

After the order is placed, Dan's friends stand up. My admirer says, "Eh, Dan, we 'bout to go outside for a minute. We'll be right back."

Dan gets a nervous look on his face. "Be easy, y'all. We don't want any trouble while my wifey is here."

"Man, chill. We got this."

Three of Dan's friends go outside the restaurant. Dan's eyes follow them apprehensively like something is about to go down.

"You cool, Dan?" Sienna asks.

"Yeah. So what have y'all done in the city so far?"

Sienna replies, "Last night we did Times Square. It was cool, even though I've seen it before."

"Times Square is always off the chain," Dan says. "And today y'all are having breakfast at the legendary Sylvia's. All three of y'all coming to my party tonight, right?"

Melody nods. "Can't wait."

"Looks like my boy is feeling you, Gia," Dan says. "You gonna let him holla?"

"Nah. He's not my type. I'm more into nerd-slash-jocks."

Sienna laughs. "Or writers who sport locs."

Now we're all laughing. They got me. I do seem to like loc-wearing writers too.

Dan's friends come back in right as the food is being served. They all have glazed expressions on their faces and red eyes.

"What have y'all been doing?" I ask, although I think I already know the answer.

"Grown-folks bidness," one of them replies as he gobbles a huge mouthful of scrambled eggs.

Mmm-hmm. I know what "grown-folks bidness" means. They've been out there smoking something they don't have any business smoking. I just say no to all that foolishness, and so should you. Hey, I'm known for random public-service announcements. Deal with it.

These dudes are not talking about anything worthwhile, so I focus on my food. Fried ham, scrambled eggs with cheese, home fries, and biscuits. Make you wanna slap somebody, for real.

"Slow down, shorty. You gon' choke on them eggs."

I look up and give him a blank stare. Thank goodness

my phone rings. I glance down at the caller ID. It's my boy Kevin.

"Excuse me, y'all. I'm gonna step outside and take this."

I rush out of the restaurant, happy to have a reason to get away from Dan's goons. "Hey, Kev. What's up?"

"Gia, you haven't called or texted me since you left. You're foul."

"I've been here for only a day and a half, Kevin. Stop spazzing out. What's up?"

"Nothing."

"All that huffing and puffing for nothing? I'm not buying it, Kev. Spill it!"

"I'm planning to ask Candy to go hang with me at the rec."

"You and Candy? Alone?"

"And Hope too."

"Something doesn't feel right about this conversation, Kevin."

That *something* is the fact that Kevin and Candy are not slick. They've been crushing since last school year, but she's only in tenth grade.

"You do know Candy isn't allowed to date, right? She's only fifteen."

Kevin replies, "We're not dating. We're getting acquainted."

You may or may not already know this, but Kevin lives with his grandparents. Every now and then he'll break with something Ricky and I call "old speak." "Getting acquainted" equals "We're in chill mode right now."

"Don't make me come home and regulate on you two," I say.

"Anyway, Gia. No one is afraid of you. What's the program like so far?"

"Don't really know yet. I don't have my first class until tomorrow. But I've met some really cool people so far. I'm having breakfast with some of them right now."

"Is Ricky with you? Put him on the phone. He's not answering his."

"Uh . . . Ricky and I are not speaking at the moment. I have no idea where he is."

"What do you mean you're not speaking to Ricky? You've been there for a day and a half, Gia. How could you already be arguing?"

"You just better deal with your friend, Kevin. He's tripping trying to tell me who I can and can't make friends with."

I can hear Kevin's sigh through the phone. "He's tripping about a guy, right?"

"Yeah."

"Remember how he was about Romeo, and he hadn't even admitted that he had a crush on you back then? You know how he gets."

One of Ricky's fellow football players tried to get at me our sophomore year in high school. It was all bad. They even got into a fight when Romeo started talking junk about me. So, yeah, I know how Ricky gets. That's still no excuse for his current behavior.

"He's still tripping, Kevin."

"Well, I'm going to need y'all to make up. You know I'm living vicariously through y'all this summer."

"Okay, Kevin. I'll try."

"Keep me posted."

Kevin is right. I have to make up with Ricky. This summer will be fun. It just *has* to be.

"Are we ready to go?" I ask when I get back to the table.

"Why you in a rush, shorty?" Dan's friend asks.

I roll my eyes. "I've got some stuff to do before the party tonight."

"What kind of stuff?" Sienna asks, looking quite irritated.

"Girl stuff. Shopping."

Sienna smiles. "Oooh, I like shopping, and I could use some new stilettos for tonight. Baby, you're picking up the tab, right?"

Dan nods. "I'll send a car for y'all tonight, okay?"

"Thank you, baby!" Sienna kisses Dan on the cheek as the three of us get up from the table.

When we get outside, I say, "Come on, y'all. I've gotta get back to campus."

"What?" Melody asks. "I want to go shopping."

"Yeah, Gia, you said you had to go shopping."

"No, I've got to go and speak with Ricky. I don't like us fighting."

"So you made me leave my boo so you could run back to make up with your little crush?" Sienna asks.

"Yes."

"You couldn't just call him?" Sienna asks.

"I could've, but then I would've had to keep looking at Dan's boys. Plus, I need to see Ricky's facial expression when I check him."

Melody clears her throat. "That was an extremely selfish thing to do, Gia. We were already there with Dan and his crew. We could've at least finished breakfast."

"I'm sorry, but I can't get back on my own. Will y'all please come with me?"

"Yeah, this time," Sienna says, "but next time you're having drama with one of your many boyfriends, you need to stay at the dorm."

"Thank you."

Sienna and Melody drop me off at the dorm, but they decide to go shopping anyway. I have no idea where Ricky could be on this campus, so I call his cell.

Ricky answers on the first ring. "Hey, Gia."

"Ricky, where are you? I can hardly hear you. What's all that noise?"

"Xavier, Sushil, and I are at the ESPN Zone."

I hear a female voice in the background say, "Come on, Ricky! It's your turn."

"Who is that?" I ask. "Is it Sushil or Xavier?"

"Umm . . . that's Tracy. We met her and her friends here. We're having an air-hockey tournament."

I can't believe I rushed all the way back here to fix things with Ricky, and he's off having fun. He's so broken up about our argument—right! "Whatever, Ricky. I'll talk to you later."

"Wait, Gia. Did you want something important?"

"Nope. I'll holla."

I storm into Lerner Hall looking for food. When I get irritated, I need snacks. Preferably something salty. Potato chips are calling my name.

"Where are you going, Princess? You look like you're about to hit somebody."

"Rashad, hey. I'm looking for a snack."

"I thought y'all were going to have breakfast at Sylvia's."

"Why are you all in my business?" I snap. "Do you know my whole itinerary? What am I doing in an hour?"

Rashad laughs. "Calm down, Gia. What's the matter?"

"Nothing!" I growl as a bag of chips falls from the snack machine.

"Well, do you want to go for a walk with me? It's probably a better way to work off your stress."

I let out a huge sigh. "I guess you're right. Where are we going?"

"Morningside Park. It's right down the street."

"Cool."

We walk in silence for a few minutes, and it's just fine. I guess I need a few moments to think about what's up.

"Do you want to talk about it?" Rashad asks as we walk into the park.

"Nah, not really. Let's talk about something else."

Rashad laughs. "Okay, what do you want to do with your life after college?"

"Seriously, Rashad? I don't know. I can't even figure out high school, much less adult life."

"You want to be some kind of writer though?"

I nod. "I do, but I don't know exactly what I want to write yet. Novels, I think, but the genre is still kind of hazy."

"You seem like a sci-fi kind of girl to me."

I shake my head. "I do love sci-fi, don't get me wrong. But I don't see myself writing it. What made you say that about me?"

"Because you're really laid back, pretty—but not a diva—and you have a boy for a best friend. *Sci-fi* is written all over you."

"Pretty observant. I'm impressed."

"That's what I do. I observe people."

"Sweet. Are you going to Dan's album-release party tonight?"

"I might roll through for a while, but those parties can get kind of wild."

"Wild how?"

"Dan's crew likes to smoke weed and drink. Someone usually gets into a fight. Not really my scene."

"Not really mine either," I say.

"Then don't go. We can chill, get some pizza, and watch a movie in the lounge."

I smile up at Rashad's cute face. "Sounds nice."

My phone buzzes. Text message from Ricky:

Gia, I'm back on campus. Meet me at Lerner Hall in five minutes.

"It's Ricky," I say. "He wants to meet me."

"Okay. I'll walk you back."

Rashad keeps on walking to the dorm when I stop at Lerner Hall. I go inside and find Ricky sitting in the game room looking perplexed.

"Gia, you sounded strange when I talked to you, so we came back. You know those girls were strangers, right? I wasn't trying to holla at them."

I sigh and sit down next to Ricky. "I think you were right about suspending the whole crush thing, Ricky. I mean, look how we're acting."

"I know. We're gonna end up not enjoying the summer if we keep this up."

"And that would be crazy. Why don't you hang out with me and Rashad? We're watching movies tonight while everybody goes to the party."

"You're watching movies with Rashad? I thought you were going to the party with your girls."

"I met some of Dan's friends this morning at breakfast. They're . . . interesting."

Ricky nods. "Gotcha. I don't know if I want to hang out with a dude that's digging you, Gia. That's just weird."

"Rashad and I are just friends. Trust me, you'll like him."

"Okay, Gia. I'll try. Sorry I've been acting like a jerk."

"I forgi—"

Ricky kisses me softly on the cheek before I can even get my sentence out. There's a moist spot on my face when he pulls away. I'm utterly speechless.

Ricky gets up and leaves me sitting in Lerner Hall, stunned. Every time I think I have the upper hand, Ricky catches me off guard.

When I get back to the dorm, Melody and Sienna are in our room. They have outfits laid out over both beds. None of them look like anything I would wear—way too much sparkling going on.

"We're picking out our party outfits, Gia," Melody says. "What do you think?"

"Umm . . . yeah. Plenty of bling."

"And that's a good thing?" Sienna asks.

"It is if you like bling."

"My boo likes a lot of bling!" Sienna exclaims.

"Well, then, he should really dig your outfit. Would y'all mind if I flake out and don't go to this party?"

Melody frowns. "What? Why aren't you coming?"

"I'm watching movies in the lounge with Rashad and Ricky."

Sienna and Melody both look at each other with wide eyes.

"Gia, I bow at your feet," Sienna says. "You are the epitome of a female mack, with your skinny self."

"It's not like that! We're just all gonna try to be friends."

"Mmm-hmm."

"Oh, whatever!"

Is that what this is? Am I, Gia Stokes, a female mack? Sweet!

★ **6** ★

Snacks? Check. Movies? Check. Two hot boys who are perfect crushes but have now moved to the friend category? Yeah, almost check—Rashad is here, and Ricky is on his way.

"What are we watching, Princess?"

"*Mission Impossible II.* Tom Cruise, Thandie Newton."

Rashad smiles. "Score. That's a great movie."

"I wanted to watch *Love & Basketball* or *Brown Sugar,* but those are both about two BFFs who have crushes, and, well, I thought it wouldn't be appropriate."

Rashad plops down on the couch and eats a mouthful of popcorn. "You're right. I'm glad you picked something else. Action movies are safe."

"Yep. I agree."

I go to set the volume on the television and feel a light tap on my head and then another. What in the world?

"Rashad, are you throwing popcorn at my head?" I ask as I pick up three kernels from the floor.

Rashad laughs. "Yes, I am. What are you gonna do about it?"

I narrow my eyes. "Dude, you don't want it with me."

"Don't I?" Rashad throws a handful of popcorn at my head, and every piece connects.

"Boy!"

I leap across the room like a cheetah and snatch the bowl of popcorn away from Rashad. I smash some of it in his face and then toss a handful down his tank top.

He yelps and flips me over onto the couch. Then he takes a huge handful of popcorn and rains it all over my head. I can't catch my breath from laughing so hard, and Rashad is holding his stomach with tears rolling down his face.

"I'm not cleaning this up," I say.

Ricky walks into the room. "Hey, Gia, Rashad."

Ricky's disapproving glare makes me feel like Rashad and I have done something wrong, even though we haven't. Ricky's nostrils flare as he looks at the popcorn mess all over the room.

"Seems like we're the only people staying in tonight," Ricky says. "Everyone's going somewhere."

"You don't have to stay in on our account," Rashad teases.

"Ha-ha. Funny," I say. "Ricky, I did bring popcorn, but someone thought it would be better to have a food fight with it."

This causes another involuntary round of giggles from

me and Rashad. He tosses a popcorn kernel at me for good measure, and I swat it away.

Ricky eases down into a chair on one side of the room; Rashad moves over to the other chair. I guess that leaves the whole couch for me. Really cozy movie night.

"Before we watch this movie, I want y'all both to know that we can be friends and have a great time this summer."

Rashad laughs. "Absolutely. Ricky, man, I'm sorry if I'm getting in your way. I didn't mean to. I saw a pretty girl and, well . . . you know."

"Gia and I are tight, Rashad. I'm not threatened by some guy she's known only two days, for real."

This is not going the way I planned.

"I never thought you were threatened," Rashad says.

"Let's watch the movie!" I say.

"No, let's talk this out right now, Gia," Ricky says. "You obviously brought us together so we can hash it out. Bottom line, I don't do sloppy seconds. I've already put work into this friendship, and I am not about to sit up here and compete with a stranger."

"But, Ricky—"

"I guess you think this is cute," Ricky continues. "But I'm not going to get dissed so you can blow your own head up."

Okay, now he's got me mad. I see he came down here to set me straight in front of Rashad. No, sir. I do not think so.

"I am not trying to blow my own head up, Ricky. You're doing a good job of it, so why do I need to join in?"

Ricky's mouth drops like I just hit him. Okay, maybe

that was a bit much. It just flew out of my mouth before I had time to stop it.

Ricky takes a long pause, and I can see his chest rise and fall in a deep breath. I don't think I've seen him this mad in a long time.

"Gia, you might think this is one of those Disney sit-coms, but this is real life, where people have real feelings."

"Ricky, I—"

"Don't, Gia. Watch your movie with your new friend. I'm out."

I watch Ricky rise from his seat, and I try to think of something to say to get him to stay, but I can't. I didn't mean to hurt him, I honestly didn't.

But I'll just have to try to fix this another day when Rashad isn't in the mix. Ricky and I have survived worse, so I'm sure that once we have a chance to talk one-on-one, we can absolutely fix this.

Right?

"Do you want to go after him?" Rashad asks. "I would understand if you did. We can watch a movie another time."

Do I want to go after Ricky? I'm not sure it would even matter right now, as angry as he is with me. I think I should just let him cool off first and then talk it out. Anything I say now will probably just make it worse.

"I'll talk to him later," I say. "We can still watch the movie."

Rashad brushes the popcorn off the couch and plops down next to me. "Are you okay with sharing the couch? Or do you want me in the chair?"

"This is cool."

Rashad wraps his arms around me and gives me an awkward hug. "I'm not that great at comforting people, but I think you and Ricky will be okay."

I'm glad somebody thinks so.

★ 7 ★

I'm kind of nervous about seeing Rashad again after our movie night. But I know I have to get up and go to class. Academic enrichment is the main reason I'm here. The drama is secondary.

Melody is still in bed, fully dressed in her clothes from last night and snoring hard. She and Sienna made it in just before curfew, but they stayed up half the night going on and on about how great the party was. I pretended I was asleep because I didn't want to bore them with the details of my night of macking gone wrong.

Sounds like I need to go with them next time.

I force myself out of bed and go over to Melody's computer to log on to Facebook. I would go into Lerner Hall to use the Internet, but that would require me to hurry and get ready, and I'm trying to wait until the last minute to get dressed.

I change my status update:

Got the blues right about now—hurt someone, and now I wish I could take it back.

Ricky never logs on to Facebook, so I know he won't see my status. But almost immediately after I click the button to post, my phone starts buzzing.

"Hello?"

"Is this Gia?" Hope asks.

"Girl, who did you call?"

"You usually say something foolish when you answer the phone, so I was surprised to hear a normal greeting."

I give a soft laugh. "Whatever."

"Ew . . . have you brushed your teeth this morning? You sound like your breath stinks."

"Hope! How can someone's breath sound like it stinks?"

"I don't know, but yours does."

"If you called merely to insult me this morning, I will have to bid you adieu. I have a class."

"Adieu! Gia, what are you on? I called because of that tripped-out message you posted on Facebook."

"What was tripped out about it?"

"Who did you hurt? One of your new friends? Your roommate?"

"Ricky."

"Ricky? Gia, please tell me you two are not off again."

"It's not completely my fault. Ricky is sending mixed signals. He said, 'Let's put the crushes on hold,' but then he's flirting with people and then acting jealous when I flirt. He gets on my nerves. Ugh!"

"I don't even want you to rewind that foolishness, Gia."

"I've got class in a little bit. I'll text you later."

"Don't text me. Call me."

I roll my eyes even though she can't see. "Okay, Hope. Holla."

I quickly get dressed for class. Even after I get out of the shower, brush my teeth, and put on all my clothes, Melody still has not gotten up.

"Melody—girl, you better wake up before you get in trouble. Going to class is mandatory around here."

"You're too loud!" Melody says with a groan.

"That's what you get for sipping on grown-people beverages. Wake up!"

There's a knock on our door. When I open it, Sienna flies into the room in a burst of energy.

"Mel, wake up! Class starts in a few minutes. You can't be late for our science lab. We're not going to become doctors by sleeping in!"

Melody sits up in the bed. Her hair looks like a bird's nest on one side, and she's got a trail of spit going from her mouth to her ear.

"How is it you're wide awake?" Melody asks. "You got as little sleep as I did."

Sienna winks. "My secret. But come on, get in the shower, and I'll get your clothes out. It will be okay if we're a little late."

I look at them both and try to figure out what's going on. I suspect some tomfoolery or chicanery (you like that, don't you). But I'm gonna let them handle that.

"See y'all later," I say.

As I'm walking across campus to the lecture hall, I see

Ricky walking and talking animatedly with Xavier. Sushil is following behind, but he's not joining in the conversation. I want to run and catch up, but I decide against it.

I thought I was running late, but when I get to the lecture hall, I'm one of the first ones to arrive. I take a seat in the front of the class and doodle in my notebook while everyone else trickles in.

Rashad comes in with a small but noisy group. He's in the middle of a conversation as he brushes by me. He doesn't even say hello.

Wow.

"Hi, I'm Mrs. Bryant, and I'm going to be your tour guide this summer!"

Our tour guide? Oh, no. I feel some teacher "creative" moment coming on. I should've known when I peeped out her tie-dyed T-shirt and Birkenstocks that she was going to be *extra*.

"Most of you aren't from New York City," Mrs. Bryant continues. "So I'm sure you're going to do lots of sight-seeing."

Okay, so maybe this could be fun! She's talking about being a real tour guide.

Mrs. Bryant says, "When you visit the sights like the Statue of Liberty, Battery Park, and everything else, I want you to take a notebook."

Surprisingly, nobody groans or complains! I guess that's because we're a class full of smarty-pants. Back at Long-fellow High it would've taken Mrs. B, our English teacher, about half an hour to calm everybody back down after mentioning a writing assignment.

"With your notebooks, I want you to journal your first

impressions of each landmark. In order to be a good writer, you must first learn to capture your experiences in words."

Mrs. Bryant has her hands clasped over her heart like she's about to say "The Pledge of Allegiance." At least she's excited about the project, and no one can take that away from her (insert blank stare).

"You'll partner up with one or two people, and you'll write what you experience with your five senses. Start today!"

After class, everyone picks partners to start the project. This is the disadvantage of being the new person. The only person I know in here is Rashad, and thank God he's coming my way.

"Wanna partner up, Princess?" he asks.

"Yes, I do."

He flashes me a smile. "You didn't want to keep me in suspense at all? Just a little?"

"Do shut up, Rashad! Ugh!"

"Wait, is Ricky going to mind us being partners?"

He most probably will, but I reply, "Why would Ricky mind me completing my project?"

"Cool, so let's start today. First stop, Canal Street."

"A street? Our first stop is a street?"

Rashad laughs. "If you want a great first journal entry, Canal Street is the place. Go put on some sneakers and meet me in front of the dorm."

Rashad walks off with some of his boy groupies. These are the guys who try to imitate his swagger, or swagger-jack, if you will. But instead of being annoyed by these dudes, Rashad seems to actually like it.

Melody and Sienna are in our room when I get there.

It's like the two of them are joined at the hip or something. I seem to recall Melody saying that she and I were going to become BFFs by the end of the summer. But looks like she's found another bestie.

"Where are you going?" Sienna asks as I put on my sneakers.

"To Canal Street with Rashad. I'll see y'all later."

Melody and Sienna look at each other and then laugh.

"You think we're letting you get away with that?" Melody asks, getting over her giggles.

"Get away with what?"

Sienna says, "Your little sneak date with Rashad."

"It's not a date. It's a class assignment."

"And you just happened to get Rashad as your partner?" Melody asks.

Sienna says, "Well, somebody told me in lab this morning that Ricky was talking real reckless about both of you. And I heard Ricky was going to the teen club with a bunch of people tonight."

"So?"

"I don't know if you noticed, Gia, but there are quite a few girls in the program drooling over Ricky," Melody says. "If I didn't have a boyfriend, I'd probably be one of them."

This is all annoying information, no doubt. I try not to let them see that I'm stressing this at all, even though I totally am. I reply, "Well, maybe I'll put on one of those sparkly outfits and come with y'all tonight."

Melody shakes her head. "I can't go out another night in a row. I have to rest. And I've got another class this afternoon."

"Rest now," Sienna says. "Party later."

"Well, Rashad is waiting for me. So I'm gonna holla back at y'all."

Rashad really is standing outside when I emerge wearing my most comfortable sneakers. I was expecting him to be a little annoyed that it took me so long to come downstairs, but if he's heated, I can't tell by the way he's grinning at me.

"You ready, Princess?"

"Yep. Take me to Canal Street."

Again, we catch the subway to our destination. I'm getting used to swiping my little MetroCard and running through the subway car doors just before they close.

"Did you bring money?" Rashad asks as we exit the subway station.

"Some. Why?"

"Because, trust, you're gonna want to get your shop on."

"Well, why didn't you say something back at the dorm?"

"Because we're supposed to be doing our class assignment."

I'm about to give Rashad a serious eye roll, but something else catches my attention. In front of me, right on the sidewalk, is a table full of the flyest purses. They've got every name brand, every color, and every style.

The cute little girl at the table asks, "You like Coach purses?"

"Yes! How much is this one?" I ask, pointing at a little red clutch.

"Twenty-five."

My eyes bulge right out of my head. "Twenty-five? Get the heck out of here."

A Coach bag for twenty-five dollars? Why did Melody not inform me of this bargain shopper's haven? I love New York!

"Wait," I ask. "Is this real?"

Rashad laughs. "Nothing is real on Canal Street, Gia. You have entered the land of knockoffs."

Knockoffs! Boo to this little girl, and quadruple womp on me for thinking I could score a real Coach purse for next to nothing.

I say to the girl, "Uh, no, thanks. Let's go, Rashad."

Can someone explain to me why dude is still laughing? I know Rashad brought me out here just to have his own little personal laugh fest.

"What is so funny?" I ask.

Rashad clutches his side as though he's trying to make himself stop guffawing. He's *so* not doing a good job of it.

"You. You're funny. I wish you could've seen your face when you found out that bag was fake."

"Yeah, well, I hope you got what you needed for your journal entry."

"Yes, I did. Thank you."

I roll my eyes at Rashad and storm up Canal Street. I'm not even impressed by the cute Baby Phat earrings I see on my left or the guy with a case full of Fossil watches on my right. Rashad has something for his journal entry, but I do too. I'm gonna call it *Canal Street—Avenue of Lies.*

"Gia, wait up!"

I stop marching long enough for Rashad to catch up.

"You hungry?" he asks when he reaches me.

"Why? You gonna show me a restaurant with fake food?"

He chuckles. "No. It's a really good Vietnamese place you have to try."

"I've never had Vietnamese food before."

"All the more reason why you have to try it. Come on. It's right down this street."

Rashad pulls me into an overly crowded restaurant. There are a lot of non-English conversations going on, but it sounds more like synchronized chaos than noise.

My stomach grumbles. "It smells great in here. I'm hungry."

Rashad laughs. "All that storming up and down the street worked up an appetite, huh?"

"Boy, please."

We get shown to a table close to the door, which is good because the tables are so close together that squeezing to the back would've been annoying. The waitress leaves us with menus and slams glasses of water down in front of us.

"Okay . . ." I say.

"I know, the service isn't the greatest, but the food is really good."

I flip the menu over, which is partially in Vietnamese. "So what's good?"

"How about the frog legs."

"How about no. Don't play with me, Rashad."

"Okay. Try the lemongrass chicken. It's spicy, just like you."

"Don't know what lemongrass is, but I heard chicken, so I guess it's safe."

My phone buzzes as the waitress takes our order. I let Rashad order everything because he seems to know what he's doing. Everything on the menu has a number next to it, and Rashad already knows by heart the numbers of the stuff he wants.

I try to read my text message without Rashad noticing.

Talked to Hope. She said u want 2 apologize.

Are you kidding me? I'm so mad I feel like I'm about to foam at the mouth. First at Hope for feeling the need to meddle, and second at Ricky for sending me this foolishness.

"It's rude to text at the table, Gia."

"I know. I'm sorry, Rashad."

"It's even ruder to get mad at the text and then not share."

"It's nothing. Just Ricky getting on my nerves again."

"That dude. He interrupted my movie date; now he's moving in on my lunch. What's the deal with you two anyway? I feel like you aren't telling me everything."

Movie date? What movie date?

"There's not much to tell."

"Y'all didn't hook up, did you?"

"What? How is that your business?"

I stop short of telling Rashad that Ricky and I are virgins. That is unnecessary information as far as I'm concerned.

"It's not my business, but I'm trying to get to know you."

"Ricky and I are best friends who started digging one another."

"That's all?"

"It's all you need to know," I say with a wink.

Our food is finally here, and mine looks good. Rashad ordered some kind of beef and noodle dish for himself. This spot is the bidness, for real.

Rashad bows his head, grabs my hand, and says a short prayer over our food. Really cool. "Was that okay? I didn't even ask you. I'm sorry."

I let out a little giggle. "I pray, Rashad. That was fine."

"Good, 'cause I wasn't really thinking. I just feel really comfortable around you, I guess."

"Same here. My mama would like you too."

What is wrong with me? Why did I just say that? Can someone please get me some Kaopectate for my diarrhea of the mouth!

"Would she like me better than she likes Ricky?"

"What makes you think she likes him?"

Rashad laughs. "If she didn't, you probably wouldn't be here with him for the summer."

"True, true, true. You ought to be an FBI agent with that observation thing you got going."

I take a bite of my lemongrass chicken, and a burst of flavor sensations fills my mouth. I don't care if I sound like a chewing-gum commercial: this food is yummy to infinity.

"You like?" Rashad asks.

I nod. "How can you tell?"

"You close your eyes with every bite. It's hilarious."

"Thank you, Rashad. This is the best meal I've had so far in New York City."

"See! I told you to trust me. Do you trust me yet?"

"No comment."

"Aw, Princess, you make a brother work hard."

So this is a guy putting in work? I can't say that any-one's ever put in work trying to get with me. Ricky just kinda eased into his slot. He moved from bestie to crush without any work at all. "No pain, no gain."

Rashad throws his head back and laughs out loud. "You're right."

At the end of the meal, the waitress brings our check, and Rashad takes it. "I got it, Princess."

"I can pay my own way."

"I invited you. I don't invite a young lady to a meal without paying. It's called home training."

I can get used to the way Rashad treats me. We might not have the history I have with Ricky, but we've got something. A connection, a bond . . . something.

"Can I take you out on a real date on Friday night, Gia?" Rashad asks as we walk back to the subway terminal.

"Was this a practice date?" I ask.

"No. This was a sneak date."

"You didn't have to sneak. I would've said yes."

Rashad shakes his head. "I don't believe that. You still haven't said yes to Friday."

"Yes."

My answer sounds weird coming out of my mouth. Is saying yes to Rashad moving me even further away from Ricky? If Ricky finds out about this date, he's going to have a coronary.

Well, I hope he'll be mad about me going out with Rashad, because the spot on my face where he kissed me still tingles. I feel selfish about enjoying time with Rashad and not allowing Ricky to do the same.

"You said yes! Wow, I never thought you would," Rashad says.

I nod and look at the ground. I should be happy that one of the finest boys in the program is pushing up on me, but all I can think about is what Ricky will do and feel when he finds out.

When I get back to the dorm, I send Ricky a text to reply to his earlier one.

IDK what Hope is talking about. Lata.

Even if I do want to apologize to Ricky at some point, it's not about to be now. I mean, how foolish is it that he texts me about me giving him an apology?

"How was your date?" Melody asks as she emerges from the bathroom.

"It wasn't a date. Did you take a nap?"

"Yes. Sienna wants to go to that teen club in Brooklyn. Everyone is going."

"Maybe I'll roll too."

"Please, please, come, Gia. Sienna will probably end up in her boyfriend's face, and I'll be left alone."

"Do you like to dance?" I ask. "Because I can't hear music and *not* dance."

"I dance, but I don't dance hard. Are you one of those girls who sweats her hairstyle out?"

"Umm, no! But I totally could've had a starring role in *Save the Last Dance.*"

Melody grins. "Love that movie."

"I know, right."

"I've got to go to class now, but you'd better have an outfit selected for tonight by the time I'm back."

"Why do I have to have it selected by then?"

Melody replies, "Duh, I have to approve it first."

Are you kidding me?

"Ta-ta for now!" Melody says. "Keep it fabulous."

After Melody leaves, I plop down onto the bed, ready to take a nap myself. I want to be freshalicious (yes, I totally just made that up) for tonight, especially if Ricky plans on walking up in the spot with some other girls. He needs to see what he's missing out on. Truth.

When I lie down, the butterfly clip that Ricky bought me pokes me in the head. I sigh and snatch it out of my hair. I don't belong to him, or anyone. I'm just me, and I'm going to be friends with whomever I choose.

"Gia, you look smokin' hot!" Melody exclaims as I do a little spin.

"I don't know about my back being out, though. Is that cool?"

I brought this blouse from Hope's closet. It's got black sequins all over it, and the back is completely out. It looked acceptable on the hanger, but now, I'm not so sure.

Sienna rolls her eyes. "Yes, it's cool. It's not like the top is hoochie or anything. Your whole front is covered."

I glance in the mirror. "Well, it looks kinda hoochie to me."

"I disagree," Melody replies. "Plus, those boots are off the chain."

"That's my other issue. Boots are okay in the summertime? With shorts?"

"All the celebrities do it, girl. Rihanna wears boots all year long," Sienna explains.

"But won't my ankles get hot?"

"Girl, stop!" Sienna says. "You'll definitely be making Ricky jealous tonight."

"I know, right!" Melody chimes in.

"I don't know if I'm trying to make him jealous. I definitely want him to notice me. . . ."

"And Rashad too?" Sienna asks.

"Yeah, him too."

"Are you done gazing at yourself in the mirror so we can go?" Melody fusses.

I pull myself away from my own reflection so we can hit the spot. We strut down the hall like we're walking down Rodeo Drive or something, looking fierce as what!

When the elevator door opens, it's already half full with some girls from upstairs. We squeeze in, though, because we don't feel like waiting for the next one.

"Hey, Tracy," Melody says to one of the girls. "Where are y'all going?"

Tracy? As in Tracy from ESPN Zone? Hmmm . . . me no likey.

"To the teen club in Brooklyn," Tracy replies. "Y'all too?"

"Yes, Y'all wanna ride the subway with us?"

Tracy shakes her head. "No, because we've got to wait on our guys."

The other two girls with Tracy giggle like they've got

an inside joke. So I've gotta ask, "What is so funny about waiting for boys?"

"They're just giggling because I'm going with Ricky Freeman and they think you'll be angry."

I lift an eyebrow. "Why would I be angry?"

"You're not? Aren't you Gia? You're the one who called when we were at the ESPN Zone, right?"

"I don't know what Ricky told you, but he and I are just friends."

"Oh. Well, he made it seem like you were crushing on him, that's all."

Okay, so I'm smart enough to know when a girl is running game. I've learned game from the best of the best. But it still annoys me that Ricky would have a conversation about me with anyone else. And are they really going to the club together?

"He's so silly!" I reply.

Tracy looks confused, so that means I've handled my bidness properly. Can't have these girls thinking they've got me stressed.

Even if I'm totally stressed.

When the elevator doors open, Ricky and Xavier are waiting in the lobby. Ricky looks at all of us, with a very uncomfortable look of his own.

"Hey, Ricky," I say. "I met your new friend on the elevator. Tracy says you two are going to the teen club together."

"Well, not together together. We're just riding the subway with them," Ricky explains.

I turn and cheese at Tracy. "Is that all? Tracy made it sound like a date."

"No, I didn't," Tracy whispers.

I lean toward Tracy and cup my hand to my ear. "What was that you said?"

"I said that I never said it was a date."

I shrug. "Oh, I must have heard you wrong. Since you're all just riding the subway together, we'll go along too."

Ricky's face bursts into a smile. "Cool!"

Ha!!! Tracy doesn't want it with me!

We all ride the subway and walk a few blocks to this hip warehouse-type spot. It's huge and has three levels all for our partying pleasure.

As we stand in line, Ricky and Xavier hang back like they're not really with our group. I don't know what that's about, but it probably has something to do with the mean side-eye combinations coming from both me and Tracy.

Once we're on the inside, and there's tons of people around, Ricky taps me on the shoulder and pulls me to the side. "Where's your friend?" he asks.

"Rashad? Don't know. Didn't invite him."

"You do know I'm definitely not on a date with Tracy."

I nod. "I understood it the first time you said it. Anything else?"

"You look good."

Dang my hide! Why am I smiling? I'm supposed to be punishing him with indifference! "Thanks. You too," I reply, totally against my will.

"So you want to dance?"

I give Ricky a mischievous grin. "No, but it looks like Tracy does."

"Wow! Okay, Gia. I'm-a get back at you later."

"Holla!"

Melody and Sienna run up on me as Ricky walks away. "Did he ask you to dance with him?" Melody asks.

"Yes."

"Then why are you still standing here?"

"Because he can't play me and get away with it. I don't roll like that."

Okay, so that's only partially true. I will not allow Ricky to play me. No how, no way. But the real reason why I didn't dance with him is because these ankle boots are pinching the hades out of my toes.

It's not easy being a fashion icon.

★ 8 ★

I'm doing a countdown to my date tonight with Rashad.
I could barely keep my attention on my classes this week
because all I could think about was holding hands with
Rashad or kissing Rashad. That's all bad. What's worse
is that I haven't been thinking about Ricky. Not as much
as I should.

I don't think I'm a player. I think I'm a one-guy kinda
girl. And that one guy I'm digging right now is Rashad.

I'm sitting in the computer lab at our dorm uploading
pictures to Facebook. Most of the pictures are of me and
Rashad hanging out in New York. A couple are from our
first night in Times Square, and some are of Melody and
Sienna.

As soon as I post, Hope starts instant messaging me.

Hope: Who is that cutie in the pictures?
Me: Which one?

Hope: The one with the locs.

Me: That's Rashad.

Hope: The dude you were telling me about?

Me: Yes.

Hope: Ricky is in trouble. That dude is all up on you in half those pictures.

Me: He is, isn't he?

Hope: Ricky called me.

Me: What? What is he calling you for?

Hope: He didn't want me to tell you.

Me: So why did you even tell me he called?

Hope: You know I can't keep a secret, Gia.

Me: That's what I'm counting on.

Hope: Shut up! I'm really not telling you now.

Me: Well, then, change the subject. What's up with Kev and Candy?

Hope: The same. I think Kevin has decided to marry Candy. He told her they were courting.

Me: ROFL. You know when Kevin pulls out words like *courting*, it's all bad.

Hope: That's what I thought.

Me: Well, I gotta go.

Hope: Why?

Me: I have a date.

Hope: A date? With Rashad?

Me: Yep.

Hope: Gia, I'm praying against that player spirit you've got.

Me: N E Way . . .

Hope: Gia, you need to decide what you really want.

Me: Okay. Holla.

I log off the computer and think for a second about what Hope said. Yes, I would like to decide what I really want. But do I know what I really want? Not when it comes to crushes, I don't. I knew I really wanted to have fun this summer, and so far I'm doing that—just not with Ricky.

I look at myself in the mirror before I leave for my date. I'm wearing hip-hugger jeans and a baby tee. Kinda casual and glam at the same time. I thought about wearing some cute shoes, but Rashad loves walking, so sneakers it is.

I rush down the hall to the elevator because I'm trying not to run into Melody and Sienna. I think they went to a party, but better safe than sorry. They are all up in my bidness lately, and I can't be sure they're not taking stuff back to Ricky.

Speaking of Ricky, guess who's standing in the elevator as the doors open? Yep. Mr. Ricky Ricardo himself. For a split second, I consider taking the stairs, but that would just be too crazy, especially since Ricky is holding the door-open button.

"Hey, Gia."

"Hey."

"How are your classes so far?"

"Fine." I give him a serious eye roll. Is that all he can think to ask me? Boo!

"Are we not talking?"

I shrug. "You're the one who wanted to check me, Ricky. You tell me."

"I didn't check you."

"You're right. You didn't check me, but you tried."

"Gia, why are you playing games? You know how I feel about you."

"No, I don't, Ricky. One day you're kissing my cheek and giving me butterfly clips, and the next you're saying, 'Let's put crushes on hold.' I think I know how you feel, but you change from day to day."

"And you don't?"

"Not like you. No."

"So tell me then, where are you going right now?"

I pause for a second. What point does me going out with Rashad prove? That I like having fun?

It definitely doesn't prove anything about me being flaky. Because *that* I am not. This is all Ricky's fault. If he had been true to me from the start, I wouldn't have thought twice about Rashad.

I decide not to answer Ricky's question because I can show him better than I can tell him.

Rashad is having a conversation with some other kids when I walk up but immediately stops talking when he sees me. Ricky keeps walking, but I don't miss the stank look he throws my direction.

"Hey, Princess. You ready?"

I nod because I can't speak. I have a huge knot in my throat, and I feel like I could burst into tears at any second. I hate that Ricky being mad at me makes me feel like this. Why can't I be like a regular girl and have a different crush every month without a thought?

This is way too stressful.

It's like my heart hurts or something. Ricky is my best friend, and we just keep arguing. Does this mean we're not friends anymore if we can't get along?

Or maybe he's changing. Maybe I'm changing. Maybe we're both changing.

"Are we going on the subway?" I ask.

"No. It's just a short walk. Is that cool?"

"Yes."

It feels really strange spending time with Rashad alone at night. Is it my imagination, or is Rashad bumping into me on purpose? He's walking so close to me his arm keeps brushing my arm. We're not talking, but I suppose it's because I haven't said one word after hello. I'm not in a chatty mood.

"We're here," Rashad says.

Here is a tiny coffeehouse. We go inside, and the first thing I notice is the lack of tables and chairs. There are lots of sofas, love seats, beanbags, and pillows instead. In the front of the coffeehouse, a tiny girl with a head full of wild braids stands with a microphone in her hand.

"Come on." Rashad pulls me over to a wicker couch covered with pillows. "She's about to start."

We sit down, and the lights dim. Rashad politely leaves space between us. Yeah, I appreciate him for that. We're not up to the snuggling stage yet.

A big voice comes out of the little girl.

"He loves me.
I can tell by his smile.
He loves me not
'Cause he smiles at her and her too. . . .
His eyes, his walk
His gangsta street talk
Leave me mesmerized
Entranced
By his steez, his stance.

His love is life
And I wanna see him in mine.
I tell him I love him a thousand times
I love him
Ain't met another like him
I love him not
'Cause yesterday . . . I met his other
girlfriend."

The girl smiles and bows like she didn't just say the angriest poem I've ever heard. As a matter of fact, I think that was the angriest poem on the planet.

I don't know how or when it happened, but somehow I ended up sitting close to Rashad on the little couch. He's not trying to push up or anything, but I can feel the warmth of his arm as it brushes against me.

Could I be digging Rashad like this and still be crushing on Ricky at the same time? I don't even know the rules for multiple crushes. Like, if the two guys are friends, does it make it worse?

Not that Ricky and Rashad are anywhere close to being friends, but what if at some point they got to be cool? Then what?

After the poetry set is over, we take our time walking back to the dorm. Rashad slips his arm around my waist, and I don't object.

"You're smooth, Rashad. You know that, right?"

He chuckles. "What?"

"Nothing. It's cool."

I'm enjoying all this attention I'm getting from Rashad.

I really am. So why, why, why did it just cross my mind how nice it would be if it were Ricky's arm around me?

I untangle myself from Rashad as I walk into the dorm.

"What? You don't want your boy to see us hugged up?" Rashad asks.

"Wow. You calling me out, huh?"

"Yeah, I'm calling you out."

"Well, the thing is I don't want to hurt Ricky's feelings if I don't have to, you know. I'm just trying to be a friend."

Rashad nods slowly. "Would Ricky be mad about this?"

Rashad pulls me into his arms and kisses the top of my forehead.

"Maybe."

"Would he be mad about this?"

I close my eyes as Rashad presses his lips into mine. It's nice. So nice that I don't care who sees us right about now. Not even Ricky.

He pulls away first. "Good night, Gia."

"Night."

My lips are still tingling when I walk into my room.

The tingling stops when I notice Sienna sprawled across Melody's bed again.

"Gia, I'm so glad you're back. Can you help me try to wake her up?"

"Wake her up? Why is she asleep in our room?"

"We went to a hotel party for Dan's producer, and they had lots of alcohol. I think she had too much to drink."

"Ya think?"

Melody sighs. "Gia, just help me get her to her own

room. It's almost curfew, and I don't want her to get in trouble."

I try to help Melody lift Sienna. The girl is kinda thick, so it's not an easy task.

I ask, "Are you sure she just had alcohol? I've never heard of someone being this gone. She's completely unconscious. Maybe we should tell somebody. What if she has alcohol poisoning?"

"Gia, she'll be fine. She just needs to sleep it off. If we tell, she's gonna get kicked out of the program."

"I don't know, Melody. Won't we get in trouble if we don't tell?"

"She's got scholarship money riding on this, Gia."

"Okay, come on then."

We finally get her to stand up, but we're practically dragging her because her legs aren't moving on their own.

Halfway down the hall, we run into Ricky and Sushil.

"What are y'all doing?" Ricky asks.

"Trying to get Sienna to her room before an RA sees us."

"Is she drunk?" Sushil asks.

"Shil—come on!"

Between the four of us—mostly the boys—we get Sienna to her room. Finally, as her roommate opens the door, Sienna wakes up and vomits all over the floor.

I close my eyes and gag. "I gotta go, Melody. I don't do vomit."

Ricky, Sushil, and I abandon Melody as she cleans up Sienna's mess. I mean, what is the whole point of getting drunk if throwing up is part of the deal? How is that fun?

"Gia, we're going to see the Statue of Liberty tomorrow. Wanna come?" Sushil asks.

I look at Ricky. "Do you want me to come?"

He shrugs. "I don't care if you come."

"You want her to come, Ricky. Stop trying to be cantankerous," Sushil fusses.

Cantankerous? Okay, Sushil is officially the summertime version of Kevin.

"We want you to come, Gia," Sushil continues. "Just you and maybe Melody, but not . . ."

I narrow my eyes. "Not Rashad?"

"I'm sure he's seen it already," Ricky says. "It'll be okay."

"Okay, I'll go. What time?"

Sushil says, "In the morning. We have to get there early, or we'll be in line forever and not be able to get a ticket to go inside the statue."

"All right then, see y'all tomorrow."

So I guess Ricky hasn't given up on our friendship. So guess what? I'm not giving up on him either.

But Sushil . . . umm, yeah. He can go on with his oldie talk.

★ 9 ★

Somebody should've told me that by "early," Sushil meant the crack-of-dawn, before-the-sun-comes-up early. I am so not amused at the wake-up call I receive at 6:30 AM that jars me out of a great dream. Rashad and I were sailing on one of those water streets in Italy on a little boat. For some reason, my friend Kevin was the one driving the boat, and he was mean-mugging me the entire ride.

Unenthusiastically, I pull myself out of the bed and start searching for an outfit. It's going to be jean shorts and layered tank tops today. It's hot as what! The weatherman said it was gonna be in the nineties for a week!

"What are you doing, Gia?" Melody asks. She peers at me through sleepy, angry eyes.

"I'm getting ready to go see the Statue of Liberty."

"With Rashad?"

"No. With Ricky. Sushil and Xavier are coming too."

"Oh. I asked because Sienna's roommate saw you kissing Rashad in the lobby last night. I thought you two must've made it official or something."

I roll my eyes. "Ooo, y'all really need to get some business! How is it that your girl was passed out drunk, but y'all found time to talk about my situation?"

"I don't know. I'm sorry, Gia."

She gives me this pitiful look that makes me think she really is sorry. Now I feel bad for going in on her like that.

"It's cool, Melody. You wanna hang with us today? I'm not trying to be the only girl with all those hardheads."

"Yeah, I do. I've seen the Statue of Liberty, but it's still fun."

"We don't roll VIP style like Sienna though. Is that okay with you?"

"All that VIP stuff is not all it's cracked up to be."

"We've got to get ready quickly because Sushil is tripping."

Melody throws her covers back. "Okay. I'm up."

Melody and I get ready as quickly as humanly possible for two fabulous girls. Okay, so it takes us about an hour.

We meet up with the boys in the lobby of our dormitory. We all look sleepy, hungry, and grumpy.

Ricky has the audacity to be wearing the Tennessee Titans jersey I bought him for Christmas last year. He wears it well too. That powder blue looks extra nice on him. Plus his low haircut is fresh and clean too. All-around good look.

Felicity, our favorite resident adviser, is in the lobby

too, looking like her usual bubbly self. "Where are you guys off to this morning?" she asks.

"Statue of Liberty," Sushil says. His tone is extra impatient.

"There were reports last night of some people coming into the dorm intoxicated," Felicity says. "I'm not going to ask if you guys know anything about it, but please remember the conduct code you signed."

We all nod in agreement. Melody looks completely terrified, like she's gonna crack and spill the beans any second. I don't think Sienna's secret is safe with her.

We walk toward the subway station, but Melody and I let the boys go ahead of us. Melody still has a concerned look on her face, like she wants to talk.

"I wonder if Sienna is awake," I say out loud.

"I'm sure she's not. She was way gone last night. I think she took something else, or someone slipped something in her drink."

"Are you serious? Why didn't you tell me about that last night?"

Melody bites her lip and sighs. "Because I thought you would want to tell if you knew the whole story."

"You're right. I would've."

Ricky jogs back to me and Melody, and he links arms with me. What's up with this? Ricky is one hundred percent against random public displays of affection.

"How was your date with Rashad?" he asks.

Weird! How do I answer a question from one crush about my date with my other crush? Yes, a ridiculous concept indeed. Crushes are not allowed to inquire about one another. "It was fine, Ricky."

"Did you make out?"

"Ricky!"

He bursts into nervous laughter. Melody gives us both a mad dose of side eye and skips up to talk to Xavier and Sushil. I guess she wants to give us some space, but I don't even know if I want any space with this crazy-acting Ricky.

"I'm messing with you, Gia," Ricky says.

"Why?"

"Why what?"

"Why are you messing with me?"

"Because you're my bestie, and I can."

"Oh."

"Have you thought about senior year, Gia?"

"What about senior year?"

"You know. Homecoming, prom, graduation."

"Oh, that stuff. Yeah, I know it's coming, but I can't say I've been thinking about it."

"Well, I have," Ricky says.

The tone in his voice concerns me. He's serious all of a sudden, and all traces of the laughter he had a few minutes ago have disappeared.

"I was planning on doing all that stuff together," Ricky continues. "Me and you."

"I guess I was too. What's changed?"

"Gia, I don't think I can go back to where we were if I have to spend all summer looking at you and Rashad all booed up."

"We are not booed up, Ricky. You're so exaggerating."

Ricky crosses his arms over his chest and scrunches his eyebrows down. He only does this when he's mad.

"Gia, you had his tongue down your throat right in the dorm lobby where everyone could see you."

"There you go exaggerating again. His tongue was not down my throat."

"But you were kissing though."

"We kissed. Once. It wasn't all like that though, Ricky, and I sure didn't plan anything like that."

Ricky has a hurt look on his face, like I've just completely torn him up. He doesn't continue the conversation though, because we've caught up with the others at the subway station.

I feel sad that Ricky is hurt right now. For real. And now I'm back thinking about what Hope asked me. What do I really want?

I do want for senior year to be hot! And I'm pretty sure I want it to be all about Ricky and me. But the summer is shaping up to be all about Rashad and Gia.

I've never met another boy like Rashad. He's completely intellectual and still fly all at the same time. He's so much more mature than Ricky and Kevin and all the other boys I know. I'm afraid if I spend the whole summer getting close to Rashad, all my feelings for Ricky are going to fade away.

The feelings are still there. I can't deny that, even as I watch Ricky dash through the subway car doors and slam into a seat. He's so fine and comfortable. Like, I don't have to second-guess myself with Ricky.

I steal another glance at Ricky, who's sitting across from me on the train. He seems to be daydreaming now, staring into space and biting his bottom lip in that cute way he does when he's thinking hard.

My hand goes up to touch where Ricky kissed me on my cheek. I still remember how strange and wonderful it felt. But it didn't compare to the rush I got when Rashad kissed me. It might not be a fair comparison though. A peck on the cheek and a mouth-to-mouth are two totally different things.

And Ricky would never put his lips on mine without my permission.

"What are you thinking about, Ricky?" I ask.

"Wouldn't you like to know."

Melody laughs out loud. "Duh! Isn't that why she asked?"

"I know! Get him straight, Melody," I say with a laugh.

Ricky replies, "Actually, I'm thinking about how I should still be sleeping right now. Sushil!"

"You all will definitely thank me when you see how long we *won't* have to wait in line." Is it just me, or does Sushil's accent get even more clipped and short when he's irritated? Methinks he doesn't like being called out.

Xavier says, "Did y'all eat breakfast? I'm starved."

"We didn't eat, but you ate two bagels with cream cheese and jelly on the way out, Xavier," Sushil replies.

Xavier scoffs. "That was not breakfast! That was a prebreakfast snack."

As they chat, my mind drifts to a vision of senior prom. Ricky and I and Hope and Kevin and their dates are all in our formal attire, about to get in our limo. We start to take pictures, but when I step up to pose with Ricky, out of nowhere another girl in a prom dress steps up. She has a bodacious body and long hair that cascades over her shoulders. She looks like a real-life video vixen. She puckers her lips and kisses Ricky's cheek, and he cheeses hard, like he's really digging her.

Yes, my imagination is off the chain. But was it really my imagination, or did I just have one of those *That's So Raven* visions of the future?

I roll my eyes at Ricky as we stand to get off the subway car at the South Ferry stop. He puts both his hands in the air like he's asking *What?*

I narrow my eyes and glare. "You know what you did."

Ricky laughs. "Gia, you are a weirdy."

"Whatever, dude."

Sushil is the leader of this expedition. We follow him through Battery Park to the ticket counter for the Circle Line ferry that will take us to see the statue and Ellis Island. It's only nine in the morning, and people are already lining up for the ferry.

Sushil points to where we have to stand in line. "The line isn't very long yet, but in an hour or so it will be crazy. You'll be thanking me for getting you up so early."

Xavier pats his stomach. "My stomach does not agree. It said it would gladly pay you Tuesday for a hamburger today."

All this talk about food from Xavier is making me hungry too. As we stand in line waiting for our turn, the smells of warm cashews tickle my nose.

"Don't you want some cashews, Gia?" Xavier asks. "I can see the longing in your eyes. I recognize hunger anywhere."

I chuckle. "Yeah, Xavier. I'll split some with you."

"Gia, take a picture of us!" Melody yells. She, Sushil, and Ricky are posing with a person dressed up like the Statue of Liberty.

I take the picture of them with my phone, but I can't stop thinking about Ricky and the imaginary girl. How could he play me like that, even in my imagination?

Yeah, yeah. I *am* somewhat playing him with Rashad, but that's totally different. I didn't deliberately start liking Rashad. It just kinda happened.

And, honestly, even though at the present time Ricky is getting on my nerves, I'm still crushing on him too. Especially when he wears clothes I purchased. Dang him and that Titans jersey.

Melody interrupts my thoughts. "So, next Friday there's going to be this huge party for Dan Tropez at the Oasis. A lot of record producers and artists are gonna be there. Jay-Z is even supposed to show up."

I lift my eyebrow and stare Melody down. "I'm not trying to go to one of *his* parties."

"Did you say Jay-Z was gonna be at this party?" Ricky asks.

"He's supposed to be there. That's what Sienna says."

"Well, then, I'm going. That sounds like it's gonna be jumping."

I laugh. "Ricky, you're kicking it *hard* up here aren't you? I never knew you partied so hard?"

"Stop trying to make me out to be lame. And you know you wanna go too. Because wherever Jay-Z is . . ."

"I know. Ms. House of Deréon herself!" I say with a grin.

Truth, I stan hard for Beyoncé. Any time Mrs. Carter and her husband are part of the conversation, I'm down. I can't stand Ricky for bringing that up, though.

"Sienna says she can get us all in the VIP suite too," Melody says.

"Is she still with Dan? How is she getting us in the VIP suite if he's leaving parties with other chicks?"

"That's just how they do. They fight, break up, and then get back together," Melody explains. "But she got VIP tickets from him a couple nights ago."

"You down or what, Gia?" Ricky asks.

"I guess so, if you're going. You know, we haven't made up a dance step in a long time. You want to?" I ask Ricky.

"Not to a Beyoncé song, Gia. I see the gleam in your eyes. No, no, and guess what? No."

I grab Ricky's arm as we board the ferry. "Not just any Beyoncé song, Ricky. How about 'Ego'?"

"I am *not* the kind of guy who dances to 'Ego,' Gia. You know this."

"So what song do you wanna do?"

Ricky giggles. "How 'bout '99 Problems'?"

"Uh, no. Stop playing."

"Why don't we just put together some moves that can go on any song with a tight beat?"

"Okay, I'm down with that."

I lean back in my seat, cheesing hard and thinking of a fly routine, because that's what I do. Ricky leans back too and puts his arm around me, which is kind of tough to do on this boat that's jam-packed with tourists.

This is the side of me Rashad doesn't know about. He

has met the scholar, poetry-reading Gia. But will he dig the Beyoncé-lovin', hard-dancing Gia?

"Come on, let's go stand out on the deck and look at the water!" Ricky says after we've left the dock.

"Okay."

Ricky takes me by the hand and leads me out onto the crowded deck. He finds an opening on one of the rails, and we slide right in. Even though it's hot, there's a nice breeze blowing off the water, and it feels great.

"Finally, I've got you all to myself," Ricky says.

I laugh. "You don't mean that, Ricky. You act like we haven't been alone before."

"I guess I never felt threatened before."

"And you do now?"

Ricky nods. "Yeah, I do. I mean, I'm not trying to tell you who to be friends with, Gia."

"I know you're not."

"But you are digging Rashad?"

I close my eyes and nod. "I do like him, Ricky. But my mom always tells me we're too young to like only one person."

"So you would be cool if I started hanging out with somebody else too?"

"Of course I wouldn't be cool with it. I'd feel like you feel about me and Rashad. But I wouldn't throw away our friendship because of it."

I guess Ricky is forgetting about how I watched him drool for a whole year over Valerie. I put all my crush feelings on the back burner and even helped him out. I talked to Romeo during that time, but my heart was always with Ricky.

"So you're gonna keep kicking it with him?"

"Yes, but I promise you we're not doing anything crazy. And I won't be making out or hooking up with him either."

"You gonna let him kiss you again?"

I point out across the water. "Look! It's the Statue of Liberty!"

"Whoa! It's huge in real life!"

Thank God for the interruption. I don't even know if I can enjoy Rashad kissing me anymore with Ricky throwing shade and a ridiculous guilt trip. That's not even fair.

The ferry stops, and we all get off. Sushil, Xavier, and Melody race toward the statue, while Ricky and I hang back and take our time. It almost feels like we're on a date, but I don't get that weird feeling like I'm playing Rashad.

As we get to the base of the statue, I'm in awe of how huge it is. The sun beams down on it and shines in a green metallic splendor. Pretty awesome.

"I'm writing about this in my sightseeing journal," I say as Ricky snaps a photo of the statue.

"What the heck is a sightseeing journal?" asks Xavier, who's just walked up holding a stick with some kind of meat on it.

"It's for my creative writing class," I reply. "Our teacher wants us to see, feel, hear, smell, and taste New York City."

Xavier scrunches his nose. "I don't know about smelling New York. Sometimes the Big Apple don't smell so fresh. But taste! That I can roll with. You wanna taste my chicken?"

He holds the hot, steaming meat in my face, and I back away. "Boy, I don't want any of that meat."

"Yeah, get your chicken out of her face, dude," Ricky says.

"Ex-cuuuse me! I'm just being hospitable. Wait a minute, is that custard I see? I'm-a holla at y'all later."

"I'm surprised he's not extra large."

"I know, right."

Ricky points at Sushil taking pictures. "I wonder why Shil didn't bring his girl."

"Sushil has a boo?"

"Kinda. Why? You aren't jealous, are you?"

"Well, he is kinda cute in a Mohinder-from-*Heroes* sorta way."

"I don't like you right now, Gia."

"It's okay. I promise I don't believe you."

Melody and Sushil walk up with their cameras still out.

"I want a picture of you two," Melody says.

Ricky grabs me by the waist and pulls me close. He wraps his arms around me from behind and rests his head on my shoulder.

"Aw, that's a cute pic," Melody says.

She brings her camera over to show it to me. It *is* a cute shot. Ricky and I look adorable, and you can see the statue in the background.

"This is fun, Sushil!" I say. "Thank you for inviting me."

"You are welcome, Gia, but the tour was Ricky's idea. He just wanted me to ask you."

Ricky shakes his head. "Thanks, Shil. You are a true homey."

I ask Ricky, "Why didn't *you* just invite me?"

"Didn't want to hear you tell me no."

This makes me sad. I have to swallow a few times to keep from getting choked up. When did me and Ricky get to this place? A place where we can't even invite each other to hang or just chill without having to talk about crushes?

"Come on, you guys. It's Saturday night. Where are we kicking it?" Sienna asks as we eat dinner in Lerner Hall.

"I'm surprised you even want to kick it, Sienna," I reply. "You were a hot mess last night when you came in. We had to drag your intoxicated behind back to your dorm."

"Oh, yeah, I meant to thank you for that, Gia. I think someone put something in my punch, for real."

Melody glances at the floor. "Do you remember anything from last night? Because we got separated for a while."

"I remember talking to Dan's boy Emerge about singing something on some background tracks in the studio."

"You can sing?" I ask. "I didn't know that."

"That's actually how I met Dan. I sang at this karaoke

thing here last summer, and a talent scout came up to me and started a conversation."

Melody clears her throat. "Back to what I asked you. Do you remember anything about what happened after that?"

"It's all good. I'm cool."

"Dan left the party, Sienna," Melody says. "With a girl. I thought you two were fighting or something."

Sienna's eyes widen. "What do you mean he left with a girl?"

Melody slaps herself in the head. "I shouldn't have told you that. You don't remember any of it, do you?"

"Well, all boys are players."

"I don't believe that," Melody says.

Sienna continues: "Yes, they are. Even Goody Two-shoes like Rashad."

"I don't think Rashad is a player," I say.

Melody replies, "He kinda is."

Sienna nods. "Right. Remember those two girls last year who got kicked out for fighting?"

"Yeah. They were fighting over Rashad. I guess he was kicking it with both of them on the low, and they both found out. It was all bad."

"Are you kidding me? Rashad doesn't seem like the player type."

Melody and Sienna look at each other with weird looks on their faces, like they want to laugh.

"What?" I ask, now feeling the anger rise in my gut.

Melody replies, "Rashad has been known to be a little bit messy when it comes to that, Gia. He likes girls. What can I say?"

My head is spinning right now. There is no way the guy I know is a player. Absolutely no way. He's one hundred percent into me, which is why I'm having a hard time with this love-triangle scenario. "Is he dating more than one girl this year?" I ask, not really wanting to know the answer.

Melody shrugs. "You're the only one I've heard about so far. But last year he was supposedly hooking up with those two girls. That's why they were ready to throw down."

"They were stupid. I'm not about to let a boy get me kicked out of the program," Sienna says. "I'm not letting anything get me kicked out. My mom would go ballistic."

She thinks her mom would go ballistic? If I got kicked out of this program for anything that might be embarrassing to my mother, she would probably separate my head from the rest of my body, and that's real talk.

"So, Gia and Ricky are making up a dance step for the party next weekend," Melody announces.

"Can y'all dance?" Sienna asks.

"We can do a little something."

Sienna bursts into laughter. "Y'all be like that movie *Stomp the Yard,* don't y'all? I can see you dancing all hard, Gia."

"I *said* I can do a little something. Is that hateration I hear in your voice? Don't make me bring it to you on the dance floor, sweetie."

"You can bring it if you want!" Sienna says between laughs. "I won't be there though. I don't dance. I stand on the side and watch other girls sweat their hairstyle out."

Melody chimes in. "Exactly. I'm not getting frizzed out trying to look like Ciara in a music video. No, thank you."

"So y'all just go to parties to look cute?" I ask.

Sienna nods. "Exactly. How do you think we meet the hottest boys? They don't be on y'all hard-dancing girls."

I ponder this theory for a second, and I have to disagree. My best friend in my head, Beyoncé, is the hardest-dancing girl ever. And she got the industry's finest to change her last name. They don't know what they're talking about!

"Well, I like to dance, so I'm-a do me. How 'bout that?"

Melody says, "I have never seen Rashad dancing. I don't think he's on that."

"You're right," Sienna adds, "but he doesn't even go to the parties, so he won't see Gia there getting her stomp on."

I give both of them the hand. "Y'all don't know me! I don't change for boys. They either like what they see, or they can bounce. For real."

"Calm down, Gia. We're just messing with you," Sienna says.

Melody nods. "And what do we know? You're the one with the two hottest boys in the program on lock. I don't know how you pulled that off."

"I wouldn't say that Rashad is on lock," Sienna says.

Here she goes throwing shade again. I don't know about having him on lock, but I know he's digging me. "What are you saying?"

"Nothing."

Right. I didn't think so. This is a prime opportunity for me to use my new cardinal rule—let my haters be my motivators!

"Speaking of Rashad . . ."

He's walking toward our table, alone, looking fine as

ever. He's got his locs tied back in a scarf that matches his short-sleeved, button-down shirt. I'm telling you this boy looks like he stepped out of a Sean John catalog. He's got the swagger game on lock.

"Ladies," he says as he takes the empty seat at our table.

"Hey, Rashad. Where have you been all weekend? You've been ghost," Sienna says.

He shrugs. "Been hanging out with some friends of mine in Brooklyn. What y'all been up to?"

"Saw the Statue of Liberty today," I reply. "It was off the chain."

He grins. "I've been meaning to take you for a walk in Battery Park. We can go next week because I want to show you the World Trade Center site."

"What's up with all the sightseeing dates, Rashad?" Sienna asks. "Don't you do parties?"

"Why, Sienna? Are you inviting me to one?"

"Yes. Next weekend we're going to a huge party at the Oasis. Jay-Z is supposed to be there."

Why is she bringing up this party to Rashad? She already knows I'm gonna be rolling with Ricky that night. This is just hateration to infinity. I'm starting to think she's my competition and not some other random girl.

"Wow, Jay-Z, huh? I'll go if Gia is gonna be my date. I can't roll up in a party like that without a beautiful girl on my arm."

Crap! How do I answer this without messing up everything in my neat little triangle? I could strangle Sienna because I know she knew exactly what she was doing. I cannot stand her right now. "I told Ricky I was gonna roll with him that night, Rashad. We're making up some dance moves for the party."

Rashad lifts his eyebrows in surprise. "Dance moves? Wow. I didn't see that one coming."

I can't really read his reaction. He looks surprised but not disappointed that I would be making up dance moves. Maybe he's just stunned that I can't be his date for the party.

"You can take me," Melody says. "My boyfriend isn't here, and I don't want to show up alone either."

"That'll be cool, if Gia is okay with it," Rashad says.

I couldn't wipe this smile off my face if I wanted to. "Of course I don't mind. As long as you're not trying to hook up with her!"

"Look at you, Princess. Making demands. You trying to be my wifey?"

This wifey phenomenon is something I don't fully understand. Does wifey mean I'm the number-one girlfriend or the girlfriend who hooks up? I don't know. And because I don't know, I cannot agree to such a thing.

"Wifey? Hmm . . . I don't know about that," I reply.

Rashad chuckles. "I love when you play hard, Gia."

"Thank you." That was a compliment, right?

Sienna looks completely heated! Why is she mad that Rashad is over here at this table openly digging me? I wonder if there is some history there that someone isn't telling me.

"So, Gia, I didn't come over here to talk about parties. I came to invite you to church tomorrow."

"Really?"

"Yes. A friend of mine dances at the Allen Cathedral in

Jamaica, Queens. They're doing this huge production tomorrow, and I thought you'd like it."

Sienna frowns. "Jamaica is far from here, Rashad."

"We'll have to take two trains and a bus," Rashad explains. "You up for the adventure, Princess?"

"Sure! What time do we leave in the morning?"

"The last service starts at eleven fifteen, so we probably need to leave around nine thirty. You don't have to get really dressed up either."

Sienna pouts. "Rashad, why didn't you invite us to church too?"

"Nobody really needs to be invited to church, Sienna. It's open to the public. But I didn't ask you, because you usually go out kicking it on Saturday. I didn't know you'd be up in the morning."

"I can get up," Sienna says.

"Well, then, I'll see you in the morning." Rashad runs one hand over my braids and adds, "Catch you later, Gia."

All three of us watch as Rashad walks away. Melody immediately resumes eating her dinner, but Sienna gazes after Rashad for a while. Yeah, somebody needs to tell me something because her interest in Rashad is not just in passing. She's digging him.

Sienna rolls her eyes at me. "What is it about you? You're not that fly."

"Why are you hating on me when you're kicking it with a recording artist?"

"Girl, bye. Nobody is hating on you. I do not have to hate."

"So you telling Rashad that I was going to the party with Ricky wasn't hating?"

Sienna looks me up and down. "No. That was the truth. He needs to know what he's working with."

"Rashad and I aren't exclusive, and I'm not his wifey. If you want to audition for the role, be my guest."

"Whatever. Rashad can't do anything for me. He's too broke and too immature."

It's funny. She has so much negativity to say about him behind his back, but she's riding hard when he's present. This is why I don't fool with girls too much. Me no likey the drama. No, ma'am, I do not.

So why is it that every time I look up, I'm right smack in the middle of drama?

★ 11 ★

I feel like all these boy shenanigans are getting the best of me. I never do this, but I'm calling my mom because I really need to hear something that doesn't come from another teenager. Real talk: our advice is really not all that good.

"Hi, Mom."

"Hey, Gia. How is New York?"

"Fun. I've seen Canal Street and Chinatown, and today we went to see the Statue of Liberty."

My mother laughs. "And what about your classes?"

"My creative writing teacher is really cool. She made the sightseeing part of my assignment. I have to write journal entries on what I see."

"Well, that sounds like a lot of fun, so why do you sound so sad?"

"Mom, is it okay to like more than one boy? I'm asking because my friend is in this kinda triangle. She's known the first guy for a really long time, and there's a new boy who's really cool too. Does it make her not a good girl if she likes both boys?"

"Is your friend cool with you telling me her business?" my mother asks. There's a hint of a smile in her tone, like she knows I'm talking about me. She'll just have to guess because I'm definitely not coming out and telling.

"Oh, she asked me to ask you."

"Well, I think it's okay for a girl to have a crush on more than one boy, but when it's time to be serious, it should be with only one."

"But what if I'm—I mean, she's—not ready to be serious yet?"

"Then you—I mean, she—should not feel pressured to be serious. She's got her entire life ahead of her to be in a relationship, and I'm sure she has college and her studies to think about."

"But how does she keep from hurting the first boy's feelings?" I ask.

"The boy she's known for a really long time? Sometimes people's feelings get hurt whether we mean for that to happen or not. I think she should just let her old friend know the new one is not coming to replace him and that there's room enough in her heart for her to like both of them."

"Okay."

My mother clears her throat. Oh, no, she's about to go in with the mom advice. "Gia, you aren't up there hooking up, are you?"

I almost laugh at my mother using slang. She usually doesn't, but I know she can't bring herself to say what

she means without using slang. Not on the topic of hooking up.

"No, Mom! I'm not doing anything like that. I'm just
hanging out with friends. Ricky and I are meeting a lot of
cool, new people, but I miss Kevin, Hope, and even Candy."

"They miss you and Ricky too. Sometimes Kevin just
comes over here and watches television all day with Candy.
It's like he's wishing you'd come home any day. I sure
hate that his grandparents didn't let him go to New York."

"Well, if Kevin had come, Ricky wouldn't be here, so
either way, someone would've been missing someone."

"You're right. But I sure would feel a lot better if Kevin
were up there in New York rather than Ricky."

"What? Why, Mom? Ricky is my best friend."

"Mmm-hmm. I know all about this best-friend stuff.
Ricky's mama and I talked, and you two are more than
best friends."

"What are you talking about?"

"Gia, don't make me come up there. I'm not playing. I
love Ricky, but I will knock him out with a two-piece if I
hear he's trying to get you to do anything you don't want
to do."

"Mom, Ricky is not like that at all."

"All right. Well, I'm gonna get off this phone. Candy
asked me to make her and Kevin some caramel popcorn
for their movie marathon."

When will Candy learn that my mother is not capable
of making anything delicious come out of the kitchen?
I've seen her do inhumane things to hot dogs and turn
macaroni and cheese out of the box into unrecognizable
goo. "Okay, Mom."

"Oh, and I think you should stick with Ricky, honey. I'm sure the new boy is nice and probably handsome, but Ricky knows you through the good, bad, and ugly. Don't throw all that away."

I gulp. "Mom . . ."

"You don't have to answer me, Gia. I know what it is. I'm glad you called me. Love you."

"Love you too, Mom."

Can I just say that now I'm more confused than ever? Of course my mom wants me to kick Rashad to the curb. She doesn't *know* him. She knows and loves Ricky, so her opinion is biased.

Argh!

It looks like I'm going to have to figure out this one on my own.

"Speak."

"Hey, Gia. It's me, Candy."

"I've been waiting for you to call me. What's up with you and Kev?"

I can hear through the phone Candy suck her teeth. "Aren't you going to ask me how I'm doing, and how things are going at home?"

I answer her questions with silence. She knows what it is.

"Gia, you get on my nerves! Ugh!"

"Are you gonna answer my question or not? If not, I've got some bidness I can be taking care of right now."

Candy laughs. "What bidness, Gia? You know you don't have any bidness!"

"Pressing the "end" button on my phone in four . . . three . . . two—"

"Okay, okay! I'll tell you about Kevin."

"Spill."

"So, I've been thinking he's kinda cute."

"This is not news, Candy."

"Dang! Can you let me finish?"

"You may continue."

"Anyway, since you and Ricky have been gone, I've been spending time with him, and he's not just cute—he's cool as what too."

"Of course he is. He's been one of my besties for-like-ever, so how can he not be cool?"

"I know, so speaking of the besties thing . . . do you have a problem with me crushing on Kevin? I know you had a little crush on him. . . ."

"No ma'am."

"No ma'am what? You don't want me kicking with Kevin? I totally understand."

I close my eyes tightly and shake my head. I feel a foolishness headache coming on. "No, Candy. Stop playing. I have never had a crush on Kevin. That was him lovin' me. Don't get it twisted."

"So are you saying you don't care if we kick it?" Candy asks.

Is that impatience I hear in her tone? She's got a lot of nerve, since she's the one calling me with ridiculousness. The nerve.

"I don't care, but what about the 'rents? Gwen is one hundred percent against teen dating, and your dad is even worse."

Candy chuckles. "You don't have to worry about that part. I got this."

I roll my eyes even though Candy can't see me. "The last time you tried to scam Gwen, you ended up wearing clown clothes to school."

"She won't suspect a thing."

"Isn't that the same thing Latavia said when she borrowed Beyoncé's weave glue? You see where she is now."

"Where is she?"

"Exactly."

"Gia, shut up. I can't even believe I asked you about any of this."

No, this chick did not press end on me. I was not done talking. See, I was gonna warn her to duck when Kevin says words that start with the letter P, because he will straight torpedo you with a spit bomb to the eye. But it's whatever!

★ 12 ★

Sienna makes good on her promise to be up in the morning for church services. It looks like she's told the entire crew too because Xavier, Sushil, Ricky, Melody, and Sienna's roommate, Janine, are all standing with me in the lobby waiting on Rashad. Her hating is out of control. She knows that this is supposed to be a me-and-Rashad thing, and she's invited half the program.

Rashad laughs out loud when he finally joins us. "Group outing, huh?"

I shrug. "Yep, pretty much."

It was my plan to keep my activities with Ricky and Rashad separate for the rest of the summer. After hanging out all day at the Statue of Liberty with Ricky and thinking about senior year, I know I'm feeling him just as strong as ever.

These are two worlds that are not supposed to meet!

"Let's go then," Rashad says.

He sounds somewhat irritated, but the way I see it, this is all his fault. If he didn't want anyone tagging along, he shouldn't have asked me to go in front of them. He's the one who put everyone in our business.

On the subway, I choose a safe seat between Melody and Xavier. I want to sit next to Rashad, but I wouldn't dare throw that in Ricky's face.

"So, Ricky, Gia tells me you play football at your school back home," Rashad says.

"Yeah, I do."

"What position do you play?"

"QB one."

Rashad laughs. "Sorry, I don't speak jock. What's that?"

"I'm the starting quarterback."

"Gotcha."

Ricky narrows his eyes. "Gia tells me you like poetry."

"Yes, I do. Spoken word too."

"Sorry, I don't speak lame," Ricky says.

I scoot to the edge of my seat, ready to leap between them if they go to blows. Some girls like to see guys fighting over them. I'm not one of those girls.

"Seriously?" Sienna asks. "Y'all beefing over Gia? For real?"

Why does this girl insist on being a hater?

"I'm not beefing with anyone," Rashad says. "But I can't speak for Ricky."

"We're on our way to church, y'all," I say to interrupt the madness. "Let's think about the goodness of the Lord and not drama!"

I guess I put the mama mack down on everybody because for the rest of the ride everyone is pretty much silent. It's not helping cut down on the mean mugging, but, still, it's better than them flexing on one another.

We step off the 1 train at Times Square to catch the E train that takes us over to Jamaica. Sienna stumbles off the train and clutches her midsection as soon as she steps onto the platform.

"Are you okay?" I ask.

She shakes her head and then slaps her hands over her mouth and runs to a garbage can. She barely makes it before she spews out what looks like an entire day's worth of food. I close my eyes because I cannot see vomit without getting sick to my stomach.

"Maybe we need to go back to the dorm," Janine says. "You don't look so good at all."

Sienna shakes her head. "I'm fine. I just need some water."

"And gum," Melody says.

I'm glad somebody said it because I'm not rolling with her if she's got a serious case of dragon breath. No, no, and no.

Rashad says, "If you're sick, you should go back and lie down. We've got a long way to go still. What if you get sick again, and on the train? You won't be able to change clothes. Ricky, why don't you be a gentleman and see the girls back to the dorm?"

Ooo! Rashad is dead wrong for that. I do not endorse, in any way, shape, or form, Rashad trying to clown Ricky on the sly. It is the opposite of cool.

"I'll take them back," Sushil says, saving Ricky from responding. "Ricky and Gia haven't been in the city long enough to be leading the pack on the subway."

Rashad nods, rolls his eyes, and then walks toward the E train that's coming. I guess we're supposed to follow him and his ego over to board the train. This is not a good look on Rashad. I don't like hater Rashad.

But let's ponder for a moment what's going on with Sienna. She must have gone out last night and had too much to drink yet again. I don't understand why getting completely wasted is a fun thing for her. The girl has got some serious issues.

This train, for some reason, is more crowded than the first one, and there really isn't a choice of seats. If I want to sit down, it has to be next to Rashad, so I squeeze in next to him and an elderly woman.

"Hey, Princess," Rashad says.

"Don't you 'Hey, Princess' me," I fuss. "You don't have to be like that toward Ricky. He's my best friend, you know."

"Be like what? I don't care if he's your best friend. He's in my way. I'm trying to be with you, Gia. Do you not get that?"

"Be with me? You're not even gonna see me after the summer."

"Who says?"

"I'm going back to Cleveland, and you're going back to Atlanta."

"I know, but we can e-mail, call, and text one another, right?"

Somehow I don't believe he's this gone over me after a couple weeks. "Seriously, Rashad, what about senior year back at your school? You can't tell me you don't have a girl waiting on you back home."

"Actually, I don't."

For the second time, Rashad catches me off guard and plants a kiss on my lips. And again I'm frozen in time. I close my eyes and inhale and taste the cinnamon scent on his breath.

"Back up off her," I hear Ricky say from across the subway car.

Now he's moving toward us, looking mad as I don't know what. Rashad does back up, but he's laughing at Ricky. "Why can't you let her decide without sticking your tongue down her throat?"

"Because she likes it. She doesn't stop me."

Ricky looks at me like he wants an answer. I don't know what to say. I do like Rashad's kisses; I'm not gonna lie.

"Rashad, this is not the time or place for that, and you know it. We're on our way to church," I say.

This is the best I can do without telling a bold-faced lie. Ricky looks at me like he's totally disappointed. I hate to see his feelings hurt, and for that reason Rashad has just lost cool points with me.

We get off the E, and we have to take the Q05 bus the rest of the way. Thank goodness we timed the trip right. It would've been all bad if we had to stand together waiting for a bus. Fortunately, it's coming as soon as we leave the subway station.

On the bus I score a seat next to Melody. I don't know where she's been anyway! She's definitely not doing her job running interference. Ricky and Rashad almost came to blows on the subway.

"Gia, you've got them both open. You know that, right?"

"I understand about Ricky. We've been crushing for the longest, but I don't get Rashad. What he just did on the subway seemed unreal."

"I think he only did that to get Ricky mad though."

I nod but ponder the conversation we had. He was talking about taking this beyond the summer and into senior year. That feels impossible, seeing that I'll be in one city, and he'll be hundreds of miles away in another city. That's crazy.

But maybe this is why I imagined Ricky with that other girl. Maybe I'm the one who's gonna kick him to the curb. Maybe I won't have a prom date, because my boyfriend will be in another state.

That can't be it, can it? I really do like Rashad, but I can't see me spending my entire senior year of high school having a long-distance boyfriend in another state. That just doesn't even make any sense, especially when I have Ricky here willing to be my boyfriend.

Well, he's willing for now. He looked really mad when he saw Rashad kissing me and was defenseless to stop it. His pride won't let him do anything remotely close to fighting Rashad for me. I have to be the one to make the choice.

But I don't know what to do. I don't want it to be my decision. I just want one of them to get out of the way.

But which one?

We get to our stop after a short ride. Melody and I are off last, and I'm concerned because as we get off the bus, Ricky and Rashad are talking. I don't know if I want to hear what they're talking about. But it can't be too bad because they're not punching each other out.

"The church is over there." Rashad points. "Come on. Service is about to start soon."

Ricky doesn't look completely cool as he strolls next to Xavier, but he does look less mad than he did on the subway. I don't know what they were talking about, but I hope it wasn't anything crazy like them deciding I was too much trouble. How crazy would that be? I am a lot of trouble, but I'm totally worth it.

I walk up to Ricky and tap him on the shoulder. "What's up, Gia?" he asks. His voice sounds a lot calmer.

"I'm sorry, Ricky. If I had known Rashad was gonna do that, I wouldn't have let him. He keeps catching me when I'm not ready."

Ricky nods. "Yeah, that's what he said. He apologized for disrespecting me."

"For real?"

"Yeah, I totally didn't expect it. He said something about really liking you but that it's no reason for him to hate on another dude."

"Wow."

"But, Gia?"

"What?"

"I'm gonna need you to back up off me right now. You smell like his cologne, and that's just making me mad. How you gonna step to me smelling like another dude?"

I sniff my top. "I guess I was crammed against him on the subway."

"It's all good. But check it out: after church, you're going back to the dorm to change, and we're going on a date. A real date. Just us."

"Are you asking me or telling me?"

"I'm asking. You haven't spent any alone time with me since we got here, but Rashad has had plenty of time to make his little moves."

This is true. Ricky and I have been only in group activities since we landed in New York City. I guess I do owe him that. "Okay, what are we doing?"

"Well, I'm not Rashad. I can't take you on a tour all over the city. But we can go to ESPN Zone. I know where that is."

A huge smile spreads across my face. "I'd love to go with you, Ricky."

We follow Rashad into the church, and an usher leads us to some seats in the balcony. We get here just in time because service is starting. Guess where I get to sit? Between Ricky and Rashad.

I really feel like a queen bee right about now.

You know how, like, with bees, the workers spend all their time making sure the queen is healthy, happy, and full? It's kinda like that with Ricky and Rashad. It's like they're taking turns making sure I'm content and having a good time in New York. It's weird, but, strangely enough, I'm enjoying it.

The praise dancers start up about twenty minutes into the service. They are awesome! It's nothing like our little unprofessional dancing back home. There are some girls who are obviously trained in ballet and modern dance. Their high kicks, jumps, and twirls are mind-blowing, and the song is great too.

I find myself standing and watching the dancers with all my attention. The beauty of it makes me forget that

Rashad is sitting to the left and Ricky is sitting to the right.

I don't take my seat again until the dancers are done. Everyone claps for them, but no one is clapping harder than me.

"I told you you would like it, Princess," Rashad whispers in my ear as I sit down.

I feel like Rashad has just given me a gift, and I don't even think he knows how special it is. "Thank you" is all I can muster in response.

After the service is over, Rashad takes us down to the first floor of the sanctuary so we can meet his friends. One of the dancers runs up and hugs Rashad. She's still got her dance apparel on, complete with glitter on her face that promptly gets all over Rashad. She kisses him on the face like they are very well acquainted.

I feel a twinge of jealousy in the pit of my stomach. When Rashad kisses her back, I feel like I could choke that girl. She better be glad we're in the house of the Lord.

"Brielle, meet my friends from the program. This is Gia, Ricky, Xavier, and Melody. Guys, this is my friend Brielle. We met last summer."

"It's nice to meet you all. Welcome to our church!"

Her New York accent is thick, like she's never been anywhere else but Jamaica, Queens.

"I enjoyed the dancing," I say. "It was really awesome. Thank you."

Brielle smiles. "Oh, my God, where are you from? You sound almost as country as Rashad."

Rashad says, "I don't sound country!"

"Yeah, Rashad. You kinda do," Ricky says.

Melody adds, "You all sound ridiculous to me!"

"Right. You're Miss Boooooston," Xavier says, exaggerating Melody's New England accent.

The conversation is pretty funny, but I can't stop looking at Brielle. She's almost in a trance gazing at Rashad, like she's completely gone over him. He says she's just a friend, but I'm thinking she's a lot more than that.

And I bet she thinks so too.

★ 13 ★

"I challenge you to a duel," Ricky says as we're seated at our table at the ESPN Zone in Times Square.

"Oh, really? What kind of duel?"

"Air hockey!"

"Okay, Ricky! It's on!"

He smiles at me, and for the first time all day he doesn't look stressed and annoyed. He reaches across the table and touches the butterfly clip I returned to my braids for this afternoon's date. "You're wearing my barrette. I thought you'd gotten rid of it."

"You're crazy. I'd never do that."

I don't tell him that the reason I take it out so much is because I can't constantly be thinking of him while I'm out with Rashad. I'm not that good of a player.

"Do you want something to eat first?" Ricky asks.

"Yes, of course."

He opens the menu and then looks at me. "I think you want a cheeseburger today with fries and a Coke."

"Very good. I am definitely hungry enough to eat a man-sized burger right now."

"I'm sure. It takes a lot of energy to be a female mack."

"Boy, stop."

The waitress comes to the table, and he orders food for both of us. I like that he does that. I don't know how to explain it, but it makes me feel like a girl. Sometimes I want to feel like that.

"So what was up with Sienna hurling everywhere?" Ricky asks.

"I don't know what's up with her. She needs to stop drinking like that before something happens to her."

"What if she's really sick though? Like maybe she has a bad case of the flu."

"All the more reason for her to stop with the alcohol!"

"You ever been drunk?" Ricky asks.

"Umm . . . no! And if I had been, you would already know about it. What's wrong with you?"

"Gia, there's a lot of stuff I don't know about you. Like, I didn't know you loved praise dance like that."

"So you don't know everything about me. I think that's good, right? Wouldn't it be boring if you already knew everything?"

"I guess. I've been thinking about our dance step, and this time I want it to be a little bit hotter. I want us to almost look like we're slow dancing, but on a fast song."

"Sounds hot. What made you think of that?"

"Maybe I'm tired of seeing other people push up on you. It's my turn to push up."

"Go for what you know then!"

For some reason, this new declaration from Ricky excites me. He's never been assertive before. It's like he's always just known he had me without putting in any work. Rashad is making him rethink his whole strategy.

"Talking about pushing up, you know Kevin is talking to your sister, right? He's already picking out prom dresses for her to wear."

"Only Kevin would pick out his date's prom dress."

"Yeah, he said he wanted something reminiscent of *Gone With the Wind*."

I shake my head. Kevin is always gonna be Kevin, I suppose! I remember when just a couple years ago he was crushing on me too. I think he gave up when it was obvious who I was really digging; plus Candy swept him off his feet with her long braids.

"What's up with Hope?" Ricky asks. "I haven't even gotten a text from her this entire time."

"I'm not sure, but I think she's decided she's marrying Brother Bryan."

Brother Bryan is the too-fine director of our youth choir back home. I have to say that Hope and I both shared crushes on him, but I grew out of mine. Hope's has gotten stronger than ever.

Ricky shakes his head and laughs. "Bryan is grown. He is not thinking about Hope."

"Well, she seems to think he's waiting for her to grow up too."

"Hope is crazy."

"That she is."

My phone buzzes on my hip. "Oh, look. You talked her up. I don't have to answer it if you don't want me to. I know we're on a date."

"Answer it!"

"Hey, Hope. This better be important because I'm out on a date with Ricky." Hope squeals at the top of her lungs. I have to hold the phone away from my ear. "Hope!"

"Sorry, Gia! But you're on your first real date with Ricky! That's hot."

I guess this is our first real date. It would've been Homecoming last year, but Hope's meddling had us all traveling in a pack. Then he was supposed to be my escort for the debutante ball, but I ended up sharing him with Sascha Cohen because she didn't have an escort. Everything here has been group related. So, yeah. This is our first real date.

Yay!

"As I'm on my first date with Ricky, you need to make it snappy. What do you want?"

"Oh, I just wanted to tell you I decided to be a Hi-Stepper again next year. With you being the captain, I'm sure to make the A squad. It's gonna be awesome!"

I lift my eyebrows as far as they can go. Yes, I am going to be the sole captain of the Hi-Stepper squad next year, but there was a reason Hope was bumped down to the B squad our sophomore year. She completely destroyed a very pivotal routine with her two left feet. I only made the A squad after she screwed up, and then I went on to be co-captain. Now senior year is coming, and I'm set to go down in history with the hottest Hi-Stepper squad ever.

"Gia, are you there? You didn't say anything."

"Umm . . . yeah, so how's the weather at home?"

Hope gasps. "Gia, you aren't going to continue that ridiculous ban on me that Valerie had going!"

"No, there's no ban on you, Hope. I just don't want you to get the idea that because I'm gonna be the captain, you've got an automatic slot. We're gonna hold auditions like we always do."

"Right, and then after the auditions you're going to select me for the A squad because that's what cousins and best friends do. Don't try to play me, Gia."

"Hope, can I please talk to you about this later? I'm neglecting Ricky, and he's looking lonely."

Hope scoffs, "I don't care what he's looking like. We're talking about important stuff here. Me and the Hi-Steppers."

"I promise I'll call you back later, okay?"

"Gia, you better. I'm not kidding."

"Okay."

Ricky laughs as I press "end" on the phone. "Didn't Hope, like, make half the Hi-Steppers fall during a half-time show?"

"I'm glad you remember that because she seems to have conveniently forgotten why she got dropped to the B squad."

"What about the rally girls? I thought she was riding hard with them."

The rally girls are like spirit boosters for the teams at our school. They plan parties, dances, pep rallies, and stuff like that, but they aren't an official school-sanctioned sport. They don't even get to go on the school bus with us anywhere.

"She was with them, but she's ready to come back to the Hi-Steppers. I don't know if we're ready for her, though."

Ricky starts bobbing his head to the song playing on the speakers. "Come on and dance with me."

"What's this song? I don't know it."

"It's 'Brand New' by Drake. I like it."

"But there's no dance floor here," I protest.

"When has that ever stopped us before?"

He pulls me up from the table, and we start to do a slow dance that looks like the steps we normally do, only a slower remix. I snake over to the right while he snakes to the left. Our snaps are on point, and when we bring it back, we're nose to nose, dancing closer than we ever have.

I feel like Ricky is about to kiss me, but he doesn't, and the music changes to a fast cut. Some Jonas Brothers song or something. It's cool though because it was enough of a rush for us to be that close. I don't know if I could've handled him kissing me right then.

"That's what I'm talking about for our step, Gia. What do you think?"

I exhale as I sit back down at the table. "Yeah, it's most definitely hot."

I feel so crazy right now! When I'm with Ricky, he's the only one I'm thinking about, but I feel the same way when I'm with Rashad. How am I ever going to choose between the two? Maybe I won't have to. Maybe when we go home, I'll never hear from Rashad again, and it'll be over.

Because, for real, it doesn't look like Ricky's going anywhere.

★ 14 ★

"**H**ey, Sienna," I say as I walk through Lerner Hall. Sienna is chilling in the game room watching television.

She doesn't speak back, so I repeat myself. "I said, hey, Sienna."

"Why are you talking to me, Gia? It's obvious I'm cool on you."

"When did that happen?"

"Why do you care? Go find one of your dudes to talk to," Sienna says.

I shrug and keep going. I'm sure not going to waste any time talking to someone who doesn't want to talk to me. Plus, it's Wednesday night, and I've got to finish a paper for class and meet up with Ricky to put the finishing touches on our dance step. Only three nights to practice until the party. I don't want to miss my opportunity for Beyoncé to see me getting my groove on. Shoot, I could definitely be a backup dancer on tour with her!

I don't have time for anyone that's drama filled. Especially Sienna.

When I get back to my bedroom, Melody is sprawled across the bed looking exhausted. "Girl, what's up with you? You look like you just got whupped!"

"I went to this boot-camp class with Sienna, and I *am* whupped! Every muscle in my body is in pain."

"Why do y'all torture yourselves like that?"

"It's for Sienna. She insists that she can't get fat because she can't be a rapper's girlfriend and be fat. She's got jump-offs to compete with."

"Well, honestly, I don't care what Sienna thinks. She just dissed me over in Lerner Hall for no reason. I spoke, and she didn't speak back."

"Yeah, she's not really feeling you, I'm afraid."

I boot up Melody's laptop. "Can I use this to finish my paper?"

"Yeah, go ahead. I can't move to stop you, even if I wanted to."

I bite my lip and pull out my journals. "So, why isn't she feeling me? I've covered for her when she's come in drunk, and I can't think of anything wrong I've done to her."

"Come on, Gia. It's obvious why she doesn't like you. She's still on Rashad."

"What do you mean *still* on Rashad? When was she ever on Rashad?"

"Last summer, right before she met Dan. She hooked up with Rashad the first night of the program," Melody says.

"So you let me just hang out with her and stuff, and you knew she had a thing for him?" I ask.

"I thought she was over him, the way she talks about Dan."

"Even if she does still kinda like Rashad, what's that got to do with me? I didn't take him from her or anything like that."

"No, you didn't take him from her, but he's treating you way differently than how he treated her."

"What do you mean?"

Melody replies, "He's taking you out on dates and sightseeing, and he never did any of that with her. That's why she wanted to come to church with you so bad. She couldn't believe Rashad was inviting you to do things like that. When she heard that Rashad kissed you out in the open, she got even angrier."

"I don't understand how Rashad embarrassing me in front of everyone would make her angrier."

"Rashad didn't claim her, and he didn't compete with another guy to get her. You just took her shine and threw a big ol' bucket of dust on it."

"Well, is she feeling better at least? That's what I was gonna ask her. Was she hung over again?"

"Yeah, pretty much."

So uncool.

I finish typing my paper about our visit to the Allen Cathedral church. Then I shower and change into some sweats, but not before I get all layered in my Bath & Body Works Coconut Lime Verbena lotion. It's Ricky's favorite.

On my way back to Lerner Hall, I run into Rashad.

"Princess! Where have you been?"

"I don't know. Studying and working on this dance step for the party Saturday."

"You down for a movie later?"

I pause before I answer the question. The stuff Melody just told me is making me look at Rashad a little bit differently. He hooked up with Sienna on the first night of the program! That's just gross. And to think he's put his lips on mine. I wonder who else he's been kissing on. Ew! "Maybe. I don't know what time we're gonna finish up."

"Okay, well, let me know if you do."

I start to walk away, but then I turn back. I just can't leave this alone.

"Rashad, did you hook up with Sienna last year?"

He laughs out loud. "I don't kiss and tell, Gia. You wouldn't want me blabbing about it if we hooked up, would you?"

"Let's get something straight here. We're not hooking up, Rashad. I'm a virgin, and I'm staying that way until I get married."

"That's great. I'm glad to hear there are some girls out here who don't just want to give it up."

"But you didn't answer the question about Sienna."

"And I'm not going to. Whatever she's mad about, it doesn't have anything to do with me or you."

"But it kinda does. She feels like you treated her badly, but you're up here treating me like royalty and calling me 'Princess.' She's hating me right now."

"She doesn't carry herself like royalty. You do. Sorry, I call them like I see them."

"So what should I call you? 'The guy who hooked up with a girl on her first day in New York'?"

Rashad sighs. "I didn't hook up with her, Gia. She wanted to, but I didn't. That's why she's mad. She tried to give it up to me, and I wouldn't take it. I still wouldn't take it. Are you satisfied?"

"I guess. I was just about to ban your lips from coming anywhere near mine. I know how she gets down."

Rashad laughs. "You didn't want to put a ban on my lips. But Ricky would be so happy to hear you say that, I'm sure."

"He would. Actually, he already put a ban on your lips!"

"Well, it's a good thing we don't care anything about his ban." Rashad moves in like he wants to plant one on me, but I duck out of the way. "What's up with that?"

"Gotta go meet Ricky."

"Right. Okay. Talk to you later."

"Okay."

I know Rashad is annoyed that I ditched him and his kiss to go meet Ricky. But I'm still a little bit nervous about him and this whole Sienna thing. I believe him, but I still also think there's a possibility the story is true.

I walk into the little meeting room Ricky's taken over for our practice. He's already warming up and has music going. He's dancing to "Halo" by my favorite, Beyoncé, and looking just like he could be Columbus Short's stunt double in *Stomp the Yard*. He is killing it, and he doesn't even have an audience—except me.

I watch him dance through the entire song. His moves

are fluid across the floor, and when he leans back it's like his body is rubber. I think he's gotten better since the last time we've done this. I'm impressed.

When the song is over, I give him a round of applause. He laughs. "Gia, why didn't you join in?"

"Because you looked so hot all by yourself I had to just watch."

"Thank you. Do you wanna learn this routine?"

I nod. "Sure. It looks harder than what I'm used to, but I'll try it."

"You can learn it, Gia. You're a quick learner."

Ricky turns the song back on again and walks me through the first half. I am getting it pretty easily, and I think it's because the moves just kind of naturally flow together. It doesn't even really feel like I'm thinking about it. I just move with the music.

There's one part where I do a little turn and end up entwined in Ricky's arms. Then we do a slow rock before we separate. For some reason, Ricky keeps messing it up.

"Let's do that one more time, Gia. Sorry."

He starts the music again, and I do the step out and make the little turn. Again Ricky is late on the rock, and we crash instead of move together.

"What's up, Ricky? It's your choreography."

"Gia, did you have to wear that dang coconut lotion? I can't think, because you smell so good."

I laugh out loud. "Oh! I'm sorry. Next time I won't wear any lotion. Matter of fact, I won't even shower. Better still, I'll come straight from bed with dragon breath and everything. Then you'll be able to get it right."

Ricky joins me in laughing. "Maybe we can just finish tomorrow night. You wanna go get some custard from that place down the street?"

I almost tell Ricky no because Rashad did ask me to watch a movie. But I'm enjoying Ricky so much right now that I just don't. I didn't make any definite plans with Rashad anyway. I only said maybe.

"You didn't have any plans, did you?" Ricky asks when I hesitate.

"No. Not really. Well, kinda, but I'd rather keep hanging with you."

He smiles. "Okay. Good."

We pack up Ricky's iPod and speakers, put them in his backpack, and then head out.

Ricky is quiet for a while as we walk. But that's normal for him. Ricky doesn't talk all the time. I jump when he slides his hand in mine and squeezes. This is not normal for Ricky.

"Do you mind?" he asks.

I shake my head and answer by giving him a squeeze back. His hand is trembling almost, which is cool, because mine is too.

"I almost kissed you while we were practicing," Ricky says in a voice barely above a whisper.

"Why didn't you?"

"It wasn't the right time. Later."

"So I have something to look forward to?"

"Yeah, something like that."

"Cool."

I kind of like that Ricky didn't kiss me when he could've.

That's how Rashad rolls, but Ricky is much more laid back than that.

I squeeze Ricky's hand again. Even though I feel sorry for Sienna and everything that happened with her and Rashad, I'm extremely glad they both see me as the royalty that I am.

Sometimes it pays to be a good girl.

★ 15 ★

Felicity has called a dorm meeting. Everyone has crowded into our little game and TV room. There aren't enough seats, but there are people on the floor and standing along the wall. No one wants to participate because tonight is the huge party at the Oasis, and everybody wants to get their outfits together.

Felicity says, "I know you guys are tight, so I'll be quick. I just want to make a couple announcements and give you some reminders. Next week will start the fourth week of our six-week program, and I'm so glad all of you are having a great time. We have been getting reports of people smoking cigarettes and other items inside the dormitory. This is a nonsmoking building, and if you get caught smoking on the premises, you will be asked to leave the program. Also, some of you know there have been several cases of students coming into the dorm past curfew and intoxicated. If you are caught, you will be sent home immediately at your parents' expense. Please don't forget the reason you're here, and that's to get a jump-start on your college education."

A collective groan comes up from the group. I really don't like being reprimanded when someone else has done something wrong. This speech is no worse than the one my stepfather gave on shoplifting when his daughter was the one caught boosting.

"I know, I know. I hate to go over that stuff too, but, unfortunately, it had to be said. Now on to the fun stuff. We're doing two adviser-sponsored field trips, and we'd like you all to come along. First, we're going to see a Broadway show, and then we're going to spend a day at Coney Island."

This also gets a mixed reaction from everyone. I think we've all pretty much figured out what we want to do, how to get there without supervision, and how to enjoy ourselves without resident advisers hovering. But it looks like we're not going to get out of these field trips. They say they'd like us to come along, but the truth is we really won't have a choice.

After the meeting is dismissed, Rashad walks up to me. "Wasn't that a great meeting to have the afternoon before everyone goes to a party where there'll be plenty of alcohol?"

"I know, right? It's a good thing I wasn't planning on drinking anyway. She didn't mess up any of my plans."

"No, not yours. Did you and Ricky get y'all little dance together?"

"What do you mean our *little* dance? Why'd you have to say it all like that?"

"I didn't mean anything by it. I guess I don't really care about that kind of thing."

"Well, I do, so that was a little ill for you to clown it like that."

Rashad puts his hands in the air to block my verbal blows. "Whoa, Princess. Slow down. It's me, Rashad. Your friend. I come in peace, remember?"

"Yeah, sorry. It just felt like you were trying to clown me, and that wasn't cool."

"I promise. No clowning intended. Maybe I'm just jealous because I don't have any moves."

"I could teach you," I say.

"I'm not really the dancing type. I'd rather stand on the side and observe. You know this."

"You're right. I do. So what are you wearing?"

"I'm on my way to Century 21 right now to find something hot. You wanna come?"

"What's Century 21?"

"It's a place where you can get designer gear for really, really cheap. Everyone shops there too. It's not just for broke people."

Melody walks up. "Did I hear Century 21?"

"Yeah, you did. We're going there to get outfits for the party. You coming?" Rashad asks.

"I'm so glad you asked! Especially you, Gia. Wait, you are taking down those braids, aren't you?"

"Actually, yeah. I'm gonna wear it loose."

"Perfect!"

"We should probably go now before people get off work. It's already gonna be crowded, but it's a madhouse in there during rush hour."

Rashad, Melody, and I make a dash for the door because we don't want to wait on everyone else, but Sienna catches up with us.

"Where are y'all going?"

Melody replies, "Century 21."

"And you weren't going to ask me if I wanted to go? That's foul, Melody."

"What? I don't have to take you everywhere I go, do I? That's not fair."

Sienna waves her hand. "Come on, let's just go. I don't feel like arguing with you. I need some stilettos."

"Is your man sending a car for you tonight?" Rashad asks.

"Why do you want to know? You wanna ride with me?"

Rashad shrugs. "A ride is a ride. If Gia and Melody can roll too."

"Gia's not going with me. Sorry, honey, there just won't be enough room. But we can squeeze you in, Rashad."

"I'm cool then, Sienna."

I shake my head. "Don't turn down the ride because of me. I'll just go with Ricky."

A low growl escapes Sienna's lips. "Let me ask you a question, Gia. What kind of skills do you have that these two hot boys are cool with you kicking it with both of them?"

"Actually, I'm not kicking it with either of them. We're just friends."

Sienna ignores me and continues. "You must have mad, nasty skills. I mean, they fight over you like you're the only girl left on the planet."

"Sienna, why did you come with us if you were gonna

act up?" Melody asks. "No one is in the mood for drama right now."

"I came because I need some shoes. Didn't you hear what I said earlier?"

"Don't take your stress out on us just because you got caught out here," I say.

Melody's eyes widen, and she shakes her head. She doesn't want me to put her on blast for telling Sienna's dirt, and I don't plan to.

"What do you mean 'caught out here'?" Sienna asks.

"You're one drink away from being an alcoholic."

"What do you know anyway? You're just a dumb nerd trying to be fab. But you don't even have it in you to be fly."

"If fly is what you're supposed to be, then no thanks."

Rashad takes my hand and pulls me to the subway station. "Just ignore her," he says. "She's mad she's not you."

"But I need Melody to help me pick an outfit," I say, not wanting to leave the fashionista behind.

"I'll help you pick something, Princess. I've got great taste."

"Sure you do."

There's a train coming as we dart through the subway tunnel. There's no way Melody and Sienna will make this one, because we left them standing above ground arguing.

"You excited about going to Coney Island?" Rashad asks once we're on the subway car. We don't get a seat this time. We've got to stand and hold on to the rails. It's the beginning of rush hour.

"I guess. I want to see it without a resident adviser though. How unnecessary."

"I know, right? Sienna's making it bad for the rest of us with her drunken binges."

"You know, for a split second I thought she was bulimic instead of hungover because she's always talking about her weight."

"Her weight? Why was she concerned about that? Her body is banging."

I respond with a frown.

"What?" Rashad asks. "Am I not supposed to notice a girl with a banging body?"

Now he gets a blank stare.

"Gia, you aren't that jealous, are you, to where you can't give another girl props when she's hot?"

"I can give another girl props. Just not another girl who accused me of being nasty just because two boys decided they both wanted to like me. How foul is that?"

"Yeah, she was tripping on that."

"Exactly. So, no, I don't give props to anything that's banging on her. Sir, no, sir."

"That's fair."

We get off the subway and walk a few blocks over to Century 21. It's right in the middle of the financial district.

"Wait. Rashad, is that the World Trade Center site?"

He nods. "You wanna see it?"

"Yes. I do."

"Come on."

We walk all around the gated area where the two buildings used to stand. It's surreal that there are just giant holes in the ground there where there used to be gigantic skyscrapers. There is a huge plaque on the wall that has the names of the people who died in the bombing. I touch the plaque, and send up a little prayer for their families.

"Are you okay, Gia?" Rashad asks.

I wipe a tear out of my eye. "Yes, I just remember watching all the stuff on TV about the bombing. I was a little girl, but I remember how everyone was crying."

Rashad puts his arm around me. "I know. I remember too."

I take a deep breath in and exhale it out. "I'm ready to go shopping now."

We walk into the store, and it is swarming with people. It reminds me of when you step on an anthill, and all the ants run out in different directions, trying to put their home back together.

"Where do we go first?"

"Shoes. You've got to build your outfit around your shoes. It's easier to do it that way."

I stand frozen in place.

"What?" Rashad asks. "Come on! We don't have all day, Princess."

"Who *are* you?"

Rashad walks up and touches his forehead to mine. "Gia, do you want an outfit or not?"

"Yes."

"Then come on. I've still gotta score an Ed Hardy T-shirt for myself."

We go downstairs to the shoe section. I browse the racks in my size, and I'm overwhelmed by the different styles, colors, and prices. I pick up a pair of Manolo Blahnik stilettos. The price tag says $599.

"Uh, Rashad, this stuff is not in my price range."

Rashad takes the box out of my hand and puts it back on the shelf. "Princess, you can't afford those shoes, not even on sale."

"Ya think?"

"You're dancing tonight. So you want flats, right?"

"Yeah, or some wedge heels. But I can barely walk in stilettos, much less dance in them."

Rashad taps his chin and looks at the shelves. Then his eyes widen, and he takes a pair of silver, open-toe, wedge heel sandals from their box. "What do you think about these?"

I shrug. "They're cute, I guess. But can I afford them?"

He flips them over and looks at the tag. "Nineteen bucks?"

"Cool."

"Let's go upstairs and get your outfit."

"I just need a top because I've got a jean skirt I want to wear."

Rashad nods. "You need to learn brand names, Gia. You like BCBG?"

"Umm . . . yes?"

"I think you would look good in a BCBG top. Their stuff looks good on slim girls."

"I am uncomfortable with you knowing so much about fashion, Rashad. Boys aren't supposed to know this stuff."

Rashad laughs out loud. "Who says? I'm good at picking out clothes for girls because I love to see y'all looking hot. Why is that a problem?" He hands me a top on a hanger. "Go try this on."

"The back is all the way out, Rashad."

"It's not all the way out. Only mostly."

I have to admit the top is hot. It's mostly earth tones like beige and brown, but it has little shocks of blue and silver. It will look great with the shoes, and it's only twenty-nine dollars. But I need to know what kind of bra to wear with it. I scratch my head and look at the back again.

"Gia, what's wrong?" Rashad asks impatiently.

"Umm . . . I need a salesperson, I think."

"For what? It's hard to find a salesperson on the floor here."

I glance around trying to locate someone. "I, uh . . . I need . . ."

"Oh, I get it. You don't wear a bra with that top, Gia. That's why it's good for petite girls."

My eyes widen. This is way too personal of a conversation for me to be having with a boy I like. He's totally noticed that I'm flat chested, so he picks out a top for the itty-bitty committee. How embarrassing! "Okay. It's cool. I don't need to try it on. I can tell it fits."

Rashad laughs. "I didn't mean to make you uncomfortable, Gia. I have three sisters, and I go shopping with them all the time."

"Why am I just finding that out? Do you have any brothers?"

"Yeah. I have two brothers. I'm the youngest."

"Whew! I'm glad you explained how it is that you know how to shop with girls."

"Whatever, Gia. Come on, so I can get my T-shirt."

I help Rashad pick out a fly Ed Hardy T-shirt in about thirty seconds flat. Boys always shop quicker than girls— even the boys who know fashion-designer names.

On our way back to the subway, Rashad asks, "Gia, is

everything cool with us? It feels like you're falling out of like with me."

"Everything is cool, Rashad. I don't know what you're talking about."

"Maybe it's because you've been spending so much time with Ricky."

"Well, Ricky's always been there, you know."

"But he wasn't much of a contender in the beginning."

"He's a contender, Rashad. He always was."

Rashad stops, takes me by both my shoulders, and looks into my eyes. "What is it about you? Dang, I really dig how you don't care to try to impress me."

"I do want to impress you, I think."

"You might want to, but you're not going out of your way to do it."

I let out a long sigh. "And you think that's a good thing?"

"Do you know how many girls go through changes to be what they think they want me to be? Last summer Sienna took up spoken word trying to get at me."

"How'd that go?" I ask.

"She was horrible at it, and it annoyed me."

"Did you tell her?"

"Nah. I almost let her know she was more attractive as a science buff. But then I didn't care, so I didn't say anything."

"Rashad, you're way more mature than most of us. I don't know why you like me. I can't even figure out how to have a crush on one boy at a time."

"Who says you have to? I think it's really interesting that you can't decide."

"You're different than most boys, Rashad."

A grin blooms across his face. "You're one of a kind too, Gia. I'm gonna miss you when the summer is over."

"We won't talk after the summer is over?"

"I hope so, Gia. I really hope so."

★ 16 ★

I do a little turn for Ricky and Melody as we stand in the lobby. We're about to leave for the party. We've all decided to go together—even Ricky and Rashad.

"What do y'all think?" I ask.

I've taken down my braids in the back and let my hair flow loose and crinkly. I've got my butterfly barrette holding my hair back on one side. I even put on sparkly silver eye shadow to match my shoes. My strawberry-peppermint lip gloss is popping too.

"Gia, you look like a model! I'm so proud of you!" Melody squeals.

"Yeah, you look hot," Ricky says, his eyes beaming.

Rashad walks up. "You are wearing that top, Princess. Do I have good taste or what?"

I roll my eyes at Rashad. He didn't have to let Ricky know he picked out my outfit. He's fighting dirty now.

"He's picking out your clothes?" Ricky asks.

"He helped. I made the final decision."

Ricky frowns. "Is everybody here? Can we go?"

Ricky doesn't even try to hide the irritation in his voice. I think he's getting weary of competing for my affections. He probably can't wait until the summer is over.

We walk all the way to the Oasis club because it's just a few blocks away from our campus. I purposely don't walk next to Ricky or Rashad. I lock arms with Melody.

"Why didn't you ride with Sienna?" I ask. "Didn't she roll VIP style?"

"He didn't send a car for her, and she didn't want to walk with us."

My eyes widen. "Her man didn't have her picked up?"

"He's not claiming that title."

We get to the club, and a line has already started. We don't have to wait, though, because we're on the VIP list. At least Sienna kept her word with that. They give us neon green hand stamps that say "Baby."

"What are the stamps for?" I ask the bouncer.

"You're underage, sweetie. A baby."

"Oh!"

"How is Sienna getting to the party?" I ask Melody once we're inside.

"I don't know. I think she's taking a cab."

The music is bumping loud, and the dance floor is already crowded. We move to the VIP section, which is really just a roped-off area with free food and alcohol.

One of Dan's friends I met at Sylvia's that day for breakfast walks up to me like Ricky isn't even standing there. "Hey, shorty, you know you look just like Alicia Keys?"

It sounds and smells like he's already drunk. "Thanks," I reply.

"You want something to drink, baby?"

"No, thanks. I'm not thirsty."

"I can get you an apple martini."

"I said no, thanks."

The guy laughs. "Suit yourself. When you get thirsty, let me know."

"She's good," Ricky says.

"Oh, my bad. Is that you?"

Ricky nods. The guy gives him a fist pound and keeps it moving to the next cute girl.

"Are you claiming me tonight?" I ask. "What's up with that?"

"Only if you want me to. That was just to get rid of the dude."

I look around for Rashad. He's conveniently disappeared, which is cool because I'm really feeling Ricky at this moment.

"You wanna dance, shorty?" Ricky asks, mimicking Dan's boy groupie.

"Yeah."

We get on the dance floor and do what we do best. There's a fast song playing, and we just start freestyling. The floor is too packed to do anything major or choreographed, so we just enjoy the music and move to the beat.

After dancing to a few songs, we decide to take a break. We go back to the VIP area, and Sienna has finally arrived. Dan and his crew are chilling on big white leather sectionals. Sienna stands with both hands on her hips because her supposed boyfriend has girls on either side of him.

Melody grabs my arm and pulls me away from Ricky. She says, "I don't know what she's about to do, but she looks crazy. She didn't put on any makeup, and her face is puffy and red from crying."

It's hard to tell in the dark, but Sienna does look a little bit off. She's breathing hard and looks ready to beat somebody down.

"Sienna, baby. Do you want something to drink?" Dan yells through the VIP area. "Somebody get her something special. Get her an apple martini with an extra kick."

Dan and his friends burst into laughter. *He* was the one who had her drink spiked before? Wow. He sure doesn't get the nomination for best boyfriend of the year award. He's off the chain.

"No, Dan. You need to stop trying to play me!" Sienna pours her soda in Dan's lap and he jumps off the sofa.

The two girls on either side of Dan look offended and irritated at Sienna's outburst.

"Oh, no!" Melody says. She tries to pull Sienna away. "Come on, girl. He's not worth it."

She snatches her arm from Melody and storms over to Dan. The music is so loud I can't hear what she's saying. But it looks like they're arguing because she's got her finger all up in his face.

"Should I go over there?" Ricky asks. "Do you think—"

Before Ricky can even finish his sentence, Dan jumps up and smacks Sienna's face. The impact from the hit makes her fall backward. Dan and his crew get up to leave the area, and the people enjoying their company give Sienna dirty looks.

"We've gotta go get her," I say.

"Okay," Melody replies.

Ricky, Melody, and I go to help Sienna up.

"Y'all wait here with her. I'm gonna go try to find Rashad and Xavier so we can all go."

I go back into the club and scan the crowd. There's no way I'm gonna find the guys in here. Wait a minute. There's only one place Xavier would be.

I push through the crowd back into the VIP area. Xavier is exactly where I thought he would be—at the buffet with a plate full of wings.

"Come on, Xavier! Didn't you see what happened to Sienna a few minutes ago?"

"I just got here!" he protests. "Did you taste these wings?"

"Boy, there are more important things going on right now! Come on."

"It's always Sienna! Sienna's drunk, Sienna's vomiting! Why can't she go anywhere without causing drama?"

"I don't know. That's just what she does. Have you seen Rashad?"

"He was out on the dance floor with some girl."

"Well, let's go find him."

We leave out the VIP area, and Xavier points. "There he is. Look over there."

Rashad is on the dance floor, but he isn't exactly dancing. He's actually making out on the dance floor. The girl looks familiar, and as I lean closer, I see it's another girl from the program.

"Wow. He's really into her, huh?" Xavier asks.

I glare angrily at Xavier and then back at Rashad. I'm furious, but I don't know if I really have the right to be.

"Do you want me to get him?" Xavier asks.

"No. Let's just go. He knows how to get back without us."

I storm down the street, trying to shake the image of Rashad on the dance floor with that girl. How could I be so stupid? He's the kind of boy that dates lots of girls at once. I don't know why I even thought I was special.

Ricky taps me on the shoulder. "What's wrong, Gia?"

"Nothing."

"You're crying. What are you crying about?"

I touch my face, and, sure enough, there are tears there. Why am I crying? I shouldn't care if Rashad is in there kissing another girl. I've got Ricky right here, and he's not kissing anyone. "Nothing. Just stressed, I guess. And tired."

Ricky narrows his eyes and stares me down. He doesn't believe me, I don't think.

I can't believe Rashad is a player! He's been taking me shopping, to church, and to Vietnamese restaurants, and none of it matters. How could Rashad be a player? This is so not fair.

Shoot. Now I'm crying again.

Ricky glances at me suspiciously out of the corner of his eye. He's just gonna have to wonder why I'm crying. I'm not telling him.

Xavier says, "Do you think I should send Rashad a text and tell him we're gone?"

"I don't care if you do or don't. That's up to you," I say.

"Gia, what is up with you? Did Rashad say or do something to you?" Melody asks. "You're tripping."

Xavier says, "She's just a little bit mad that she saw Rashad kissing Keisha in the club."

Melody shakes her head. "I'm not hearing this."

"They were only kissing, Gia. They weren't doing anything crazy," Xavier says.

Not doing anything crazy! Um, yeah, lip-locking on the dance floor is something crazy. Especially after you just got finished telling me how you dig me because I'm different.

Ricky says, "Wow, Gia. You're really twisted about this, aren't you? You can't even stop crying."

He's right. I'm trying to make the tears stop, but they keep coming. I feel like a greedy, greedy girl. I want Ricky and Rashad both, and I want them both to like only me.

Ricky stares at me with a hurt look in his eyes. "Why can't it be enough that I like you, Gia? Why do you have to have Rashad too?"

I know I can't explain it to Ricky in a way he can understand, so I don't even try. Rashad is the first guy who's met me and liked me immediately. It didn't take him years to discover that I'm pretty, funny, and smart. He knew after the first conversation. That has never happened to me before. Rashad kissing Keisha takes all that away from me.

So not fair.

"Do you have any idea how that makes me feel?"

Ricky asks. "I'm sitting here with you, but you're crying over Rashad. That's foul."

"I'm not crying over Rashad."

"Then what are you crying about?" Ricky asks.

"I don't want to talk about it, Ricky. Okay?"

Ricky leans down in his seat and closes his eyes. It's late, and we're all tired. If we would've stayed at the party, we would've all still been wide awake, but somehow now we're all tired.

"Are you cool about Rashad? We tried to tell you about him, but you wouldn't listen," Melody says.

"You tried to tell me he hooked up with Sienna. He says that wasn't true. He says she wanted to, but he wouldn't do it."

"I don't know," Melody says. "I believed Sienna on that one, but Rashad might be telling the truth."

"It doesn't matter now anyway. I don't want to be with someone who goes to a party and kisses a girl on the dance floor. That's just gross."

"So why are you sad about it?"

"Because I thought he really liked me, Melody."

"Maybe he does."

I just know I'm sick of maybes. Maybe I just need to cease and desist on all crushes until I'm grown enough to understand this stuff. Ricky is mad at me. I'm mad at Rashad. It's all a vicious circle with somebody constantly being mad at somebody. I've had it!

We have a quiet ride back to the dorm. Nobody wants to talk about Sienna or the party, I guess. I definitely don't want to talk about anything or anyone—especially any boys with names beginning with the letter R.

Rashad is waiting for us in the lobby as we come in. "What happened? I looked up, and y'all were gone."

"We left. Sienna had some issues with Dan."

"What? When was all this going on?"

"When you had your tongue down that girl's throat on the dance floor."

"*She* had her tongue down *my* throat. Don't get it twisted," Rashad says.

"I don't know which was the case, but I know you weren't pushing her away."

Rashad argues. "Then you must not have stayed long enough."

"Whatever, Rashad." I roll my eyes and step onto the elevator.

"Oh, you're mad, Gia? How are you mad? Would I be justified being mad about you making out with Ricky?"

"We don't do that. We've never—"

"Oh, y'all just dance all up on each other. Yep, that's much better."

I notice that Ricky is silent during this argument like he wants no parts of it. I don't blame him. I don't want any part of it either.

Ricky, Melody, and I get off the elevator on our floor, and he walks away without even saying good night. I don't know what I've done, but it feels like this entire crush universe is tumbling down.

Melody says, "Gia, it'll be different in the morning. Ricky won't be mad, and you'll kick Rashad to the curb. It'll be cool."

I want to believe that, but I can't trust any gut feelings or hunches I have anymore. I thought Rashad was way too into me to push up on another girl. And I thought I could just keep crushing on Rashad in front of Ricky's face and Ricky would still be cool with it.

Obviously, I don't know anything about anything.

My phone buzzes on my desk as I'm chilling in my room. I pick it up to answer, but not without checking the caller ID first. It's my mom. I should've known her mess radar would be going off soon enough with me wearing back-out shirts and going to teen nightclubs. I'm surprised she hasn't beamed herself up here.

"Hi, Mom."

"Hello, Gia."

Oh, no! She's got her mean voice on. And it's like three octaves deeper than normal too. That means she's looking for a victim.

"Um . . . Mommy, is everything okay?"

"Don't you 'Mommy' me."

"What did I do?"

Why am I scared that she knows about all the fun that I'm having here? She can't possibly know. Right?

"Did you know about Kevin *liking* Candy?"

Whew. It has nothing to do with me. "I don't know. I guess, but it's nothing serious."

"Y'all are getting out of control with this crush business. I'm 'bout to shut this all down."

"What did Kevin do, exactly?" I ask, not knowing if I really want the answer.

"This fool boy came over here asking LeRon's permission to court Candy."

Oh, my goodness!!! LeRon is Candy's father, and Kevin is straight tripping. I don't know what he's thinking.

I try to contain my laughter long enough to reply, "Mom, at least he's not being sneaky with it."

"Girl, you'd better not be taking his side. This is utter ridiculousness. And to think I wanted him up there with you in New York. He probably would've been courting you all over the city. He doesn't fool me with that gentleman crap."

"Seriously, Mom? You know Kevin. I think you're just paranoid. Maybe you need to let go and let God."

"What did you just say to me?"

"Um . . . nothing?"

"That's what I thought. You'd better mind your mouth unless you want me to visit you in person."

"Okay, Mom."

"Recognize."

It's official. My mother has gone completely bonkers.

★ 17 ★

"**W**ake up, Gia! We're going to Battery Park!" I knock away Melody's arm. I'm not going anywhere outside this room. I'm too embarrassed to show my face. Everyone by now, I'm sure, knows Rashad was all up on Keisha at that party.

Plus, I don't want to run into Ricky and see that mix of anger and hurt on his face. No, thank you.

"I'm not getting up until tomorrow."

Melody snatches off my comforter. "Gia, I'm not going to let you lie here and be upset for the rest of this program. We've got only two weeks left, and we need to make it hot!"

Two whole weeks, and this horrible nightmare will be over. Might as well be a million years.

"Listen, my boyfriend is not here, and I really miss him. He's probably pushing up on some girl back home in Boston, but I can't worry about that while I'm here."

I sit up in bed. "Why do you think your boyfriend is pushing up on someone? I thought you said you guys were going to college together and getting married and all that other stuff?"

"Yes, that's what I said, and maybe it'll happen, maybe it won't. We're teenagers, Gia. I know he's up to some shenanigans. I just have to forgive him and move on if I want us to be together."

"So you think I should forgive Rashad?"

Melody puffs her cheeks full of air and then blows it out. "No! That is not the moral of this story. Rashad is Rashad, and you don't ever have to see him again after this."

I toss myself back down on the bed and will the tears not to come. "I don't want to never see him again, Melody!"

"You are worried about the wrong boy, Gia. If you need to be making up with anyone, it should be Ricky."

"Ricky is mad at me for no reason, so I don't even know where to start with him."

"For no reason! You chumped him out in front of everyone, Gia. Got him looking like a punk who runs up behind a girl who's digging someone else more."

"I guess I didn't think of it that way."

"Can you imagine how he must've felt with you crying over Rashad? From what I know, Ricky hasn't pushed up on any other girls here. He's all about you."

I feel like such an idiot! Ricky's been patient with me and this crazy crush on Rashad, but of course he's never accepted it. "So what do I do now?"

"I don't even know if this is fixable," Melody says. "But you can't stop enjoying the summer because of it."

"I just want the summer to be over."

"You've liked and lost—now get over it! There are street vendors with chicken on a stick calling Xavier's name."

Melody is pretty convincing, huh? I get out of bed and find some jean shorts and a Tweety T-shirt to rock for the day. I've been playing my boy Tweety this summer too. He's been sitting at the bottom of a drawer waiting to see the city, and I've played him for BCBG and Baby Phat.

But I know he'll forgive me. He's not like these stupid boys.

Melody and I get dressed, leave our room, and head over toward Lerner Hall. In the hallway we run into Sienna.

"Thanks for having my back at the club."

"It was nothing. I would've done that for anyone. Even you," I reply.

"Well, I don't know if I deserve it, as mean as I've been to everyone. Especially you, Gia."

I shrug. "You didn't deserve what Dan did to you. I wouldn't wish that on anybody."

"You didn't even get to see Jay and Bey. I heard they finally showed up."

"You don't have to rub it in, Sienna," I say.

Sienna drops her head. "Gia, I feel really bad about how I treated you. It didn't even really have anything to do with Rashad."

"What a jerk!" Melody adds.

Sienna continues, "It was more because I was jealous of

you. I've never been able to get boys to like me by just being myself. Do you know how few boys like girls who can name all the elements on the periodic table?"

"I'm guessing not a lot."

"Bingo. I never told Dan about any of that. He has no idea how smart I am, and Rashad . . . Well, he just doesn't care."

"I didn't know you liked Rashad all like that. You should've told me from day one. Maybe things would've been different."

"If my memory serves me right," Melody says, "you were on Rashad before you even got here. Y'all met up on the plane, right?"

"Yes, we did. I should've let him switch seats with Ricky. That's what I get for trying to be a player."

"Don't feel bad. Most of us aren't cut out for it," Melody says.

My phone buzzes in my purse. "Talk to me," I say.

"Gia, this is an intervention."

"Kevin! What are you talking about?"

I hear him take a deep breath. Oh, no. Do I even want to hear this tirade?

"Ricky told me all about you and your little boyfriend Rashad. Why are you up there playing Ricky like that?"

"It's complicated."

"Gia, this is not the relationship status on Facebook! You don't answer me with complicated!"

I hold the phone away from my face and look at it. Does he know who I am? Apparently not. "I don't have to answer you at all, Kevin. You betta recognize."

"Gia, you really hurt Ricky."

"Tell me something I don't know, Kevin. Let me call you back, okay? I don't really feel like talking about this right now."

I press "end" on the phone before Kevin gets to say something else. I don't want to talk to him or Hope about this anymore.

On our way out of the dorm, we see Sushil, and he waves for us to come over. I don't want to hear it from him too about how I've hurt Ricky so badly. I don't need them all to jump on me to let me know how wrong I am.

Sushil says, "Ricky is really sad, Gia, but I think he wants to make up with you."

Finally! A glimmer of hope!

"What makes you say that?" I ask.

"He just kept saying over and over again how he knows you're the girl for him and that he wants to marry you one day."

"He said that?" My eyes have got to look like two gigantic saucers. This is some serious talk here.

"Yes. And he said every time he saw you with Rashad, he wanted to punch him out, but he didn't, because he needed to know you would choose him."

But I didn't exactly choose him. I didn't choose anyone. Rashad chose for me by kissing that girl.

Sushil continues, "But when you cried over Rashad, he couldn't understand it. He didn't understand why you didn't just chalk it and keep it moving."

"He's mad right now," Melody says, "but it's probably just a bruised ego more than anything."

"How do I fix it?" I ask Sushil. "I do choose Ricky, but how do I let him know that now?"

"You can start by apologizing, I guess," Sushil says. "But take your time with it. He's still very heated right now."

He's heated.

Well, I guess it could be worse. He could be heated and done with me. I wouldn't blame him if he was, but if he'll let me, I think we can fix this.

★ 18 ★

Even though I wish I didn't have to, I see Rashad in creative writing class. We had an assignment to write a free-form piece of poetry with no structure or set rhyming scheme, but it was supposed to drip with emotion—the teacher's words, not mine.

I had a difficult time writing anything that didn't sound like a sad Mariah Carey song. "Don't Forget About Us" and "We Belong Together" keep playing on the sound-track that's in my brain.

I should've listened to my mother.

This may be the only time I ever admit this. She was right about Ricky. Who knows what other stuff she might be right about.

Rashad steps to the front of the class to read his poem. I don't want to listen to him. Definitely don't want to look at him. Nope. Not one of my five senses want anything to do with Rashad Moore.

He clears his throat and begins.

> "Sometimes *sorry* is just a word.
> Like when I broke my mama's crystal vase
> When I was four.
> Cried till snot ran out my nose.
> But the vase is still gone.
> Mama's moved on.
> Sometimes *sorry* is just a word.
> Like when I crashed my brother's bike
> Around the old, tall maple tree.
> Then again, I cried.
> Shouted, 'I apologize.'
> But the bike is still scrap metal
> In a raggedy junkyard.
> Sometimes *sorry* is just a word.
> Like when I broke this girl's heart.
> I'll say it anyway
> Though it won't mean anything.
> I'm sorry just the same.
> But sometimes *sorry* is just a word."

Everyone except me gives Rashad a round of applause. Are you kidding me? Is that supposed to be an apology?

Sometimes *sorry* is just a word?

Yeah, right. How about the fact that his apology would've meant so much more if he didn't have a huge purple hickey on his neck.

Sometimes *hickey* is just a word!

I can't believe I was digging him so hard. Isn't it funny how once a person makes you mad, you can see all their flaws?

Like for example, didn't someone say Rashad's locs make him look like Simba? Maybe that was Ricky who said that. How is it that only now can I see the resemblance? And though I don't stay one-hundred-percent-acne-free myself, I can play connect-the-dots with the zits on his forehead.

Ugh!

After class I try to rush out without talking to Rashad. I don't want Ricky or anyone who might talk to Ricky to see me alone with Rashad—not even having a conversation.

Yeah, it's that serious.

"Gia!" Rashad calls as I step out the door.

It sounds weird to hear him say my real name. He's been calling me "princess" since we met. *That* part about Rashad I will miss.

I stop, though I don't really want to. "Yes, Rashad. What's up?"

"I really am sorry, Gia. You do know that."

"Just a word, right?"

"Yeah. It didn't go down the way you think. There was more to what you saw."

I'm sure there was more—lots more, and it probably took place back at the dorm. Hence the hickey. "Don't even explain. It's cool. We're cool."

"Just like that? You don't want an explanation?"

"What is it going to change, Rashad? Just save it."

"Dang, Princess. I'm feeling beyond dissed right now."

"Now you see how I felt when I saw you lip-locked with Keisha. I guess we're even."

I leave Rashad standing there. He probably does feel bad, but it can't possibly match the way I'm feeling right now.

I walk back toward my dorm, and my internal sound-track starts again. Why do people write sad songs anyway? They don't make anybody feel better. Actually, they only make me feel worse.

When I get back to my room, Ricky is sitting on the floor right outside my door.

My heart leaps a little, but I don't get too excited. He could be here to tell me he never wants to see me again.

"Hi."

"Hey, Ricky."

"I have a question."

"Okay. . . ."

"If we make things official, and you're officially my girlfriend, will I always have to worry about some other guy taking you away?"

"Are you asking me to make it official?"

"Answer the question, Gia."

I take a deep breath. "At the beginning of this summer, I didn't know the answer to that question."

"And now?"

"Now I know it's you, Ricky. I want to be your girl-friend."

Ricky stands to his feet. "All right."

"All right? Is that all?"

"That's it. I just wanted to know how you would answer the question. Nothing's changed."

As he walks away, I don't know how I'm supposed to feel. He's not giving me much to work with, but at least it's something. I'm hopeful that we still have a future together—or at least a senior year.

★ 19 ★

I call my mom and tell her the whole story about Ricky and Rashad. This time I don't change the names to protect the innocent, but I tell her only the necessary information. There are some details that are inappropriate for parental units. Like, there is absolutely no reason for her to know about anyone's lips on mine.

"Wow, Gia. I didn't know you and Ricky were liking each other just quite so much," she says after I finish.

"Mom, are you going to give me a lecture?"

"No. It was only a matter of time. Ricky is a handsome boy. He's fine, as a matter of fact!"

"Mom!"

"Well, he is. Do you think 'cause I'm grown that I can't see that?"

"This conversation is getting weird, Mom."

My mother bursts out laughing. "Oh, you get to weird

me out talking about crushes and carrying on, and I don't get to reciprocate?"

"Sorry. What do you think I should do?"

"Well, boys—and men, for that matter—have really fragile egos. You pretty much shot Ricky's down when you let this Rashad guy get in the mix."

"I know, but how do I fix it?"

"This might be hard to fix, Gia. Right now Ricky is probably feeling like he can't trust you with his heart."

"Mom. I need knowledge here. What can I do to make it okay?"

"Keep doing what you're doing and apologize. No other boys! Have you apologized at all?"

"No, not really. I haven't figured out yet what to be sorry for."

"You're not sorry about liking Rashad?"

"No. Because I didn't do that on purpose."

"Are you sorry you hurt Ricky?"

"Yes. I am sorry about that."

"Then there you go. Start with that."

"Thanks, Mom."

"Mmm-hmm. When you get home we're going to have to discuss this whole crush and dating thing."

"Okay."

I am *not* looking forward to having that conversation. No, ma'am, I am not. I see a lockdown in my near future.

After I hang up the phone with my mom, I psych myself up to go apologize to Ricky. It shouldn't be hard. I've known him my whole life, and we've been best friends for what seems like an eternity.

All the way to his room, I keep telling myself I can do it and that it'll be okay. It just has to be!

My first words will be, "I'm sorry."

It's simple, direct, to the point. But will he think it's only words?

My mom always tells me to forgive people if I want to be forgiven. How can I expect Ricky to accept my apology when I didn't even consider accepting Rashad's?

Instead of going to Ricky's room, I decide to find Rashad first. I want to tell him I forgive him. He wrote a poem about what he did and everything! The least I can do is accept his apology and let him off the hook.

I don't even make it to his room because he's standing in the hallway. He looks at me as though he's deciding whether to speak to me. Understandable. Our last conversation ended in a diss.

"Hey, Rashad."

"Hey. How are you doing, Princess?"

"Cool."

"Still cool, huh?"

"Yeah." I let out a soft chuckle. I'm more nervous than amused, but he doesn't have to know that. "Rashad, I accept your apology. For real. I don't think I did before, but I do now."

"What changed?"

"I guess when I look at the big picture, these past few weeks don't really matter at all."

"You're going to strike me from the record?" he asks.

"Pretty much. Gonna use a big ol' Rashad eraser and make it like you never existed in the Gia universe."

"Dang, girl. You've got your own universe?"

"Yes, I do."

Rashad laughs, and I laugh. We both do.

"Does this mean we're friends again?"

"Yes, but not like before."

"Because of Ricky?"

"Because of Ricky," I reply. "It's always been Ricky. Honestly, I don't know how you even got in the mix."

"My good looks, my charm, my poetic verses . . ."

"We're really feeling ourselves, aren't we?"

"I'm kidding, Gia. I got in the mix because I pursued you, bottom line. Ricky just wasn't used to having any competition for your heart."

I'm feeling like Rashad is one hundred percent right. I mean, Ricky never had to compete for me, and I never really had to compete for him. But now that I'm losing him, I'm gonna prove all my fighting skills.

★ 20 ★

It's crazy, but a week has gone by, and I haven't gotten the chance to talk to Ricky yet. It feels like he's avoiding me, but I can't be sure. I've sent him texts asking to meet up, but he doesn't reply or makes an excuse.

I know what Sushil said—about Ricky wanting to wife me—but I don't see any evidence of that. I'm thinking this might be the end for us. I don't know where to go from here. I can't even see past here.

No Ricky and Gia sounds like peanut butter deciding it's not teaming up with jelly anymore. That's just unthinkable—do you know what I mean?

At least I haven't seen or heard about him with some other girl. That would make me so crazy right now.

Melody says, "Snap out of it, Gia. Coney Island is fun. Once you get back home, and you and Ricky make up, you'll hate that you missed it by moping around."

"I'm not moping around."

"Oh, my goodness, Gia. You haven't been anywhere but to class for the past four days! This is our last week here! Don't waste it crying over your boyfriend!"

He's not my boyfriend! That's the problem. If he were my boyfriend, I would be laughing right now instead of feeling on the verge of tears.

"He's not answering any of my texts, Melody. I asked if he wanted to hang with us at Coney Island, and he didn't even reply. It's not like him to be silent like that."

"Well, Coney Island is kinda romantic! Maybe that's the spot for y'all to make up."

"Right. Are you bringing your swimsuit?"

"Girl, yes! We gotta go to the beach."

Out of habit, I look down at my phone, expecting it to buzz with an incoming text.

"Stop looking at your phone. When he's ready, he'll text you. The group is leaving in ten minutes. So let's roll. I don't want to be separated from everyone."

It seems like everyone from our entire dorm is standing downstairs. I try to spot Ricky in the crowd, but I don't see him. Rashad is here; of course I'd see him. He has the audacity to wink at me, at which I shake my head. He'll never quit.

"Hey, y'all," Xavier says. "I can't wait to get to Coney Island."

"For real, Xavier? What are you gonna do when you get there?" I ask.

"First thing, I'm gonna score a coney hot dog with chili, cheese, and sauerkraut. Then I'm gonna get myself some Coney Island custard."

"All that, Xavier?" Melody asks. "Then what?"

"Then I'm gonna rest my feet and ram you ladies on the bumper cars."

"Is Ricky with you?" I ask.

"I don't know if he's coming. He hasn't been talking much to me. He and Sushil are always whispering."

Melody asks, "Why don't they tell you stuff?"

"I don't know. They act like I'm gonna tell, but whatever."

I know why Ricky doesn't tell Xavier anything. Out of all the boys, he's the easiest to get information from. All you have to do is give him a brownie, and he's singing like a canary.

Then I see him. Ricky and Sushil show up in the lobby, and guess what Ricky is wearing! My Titans jersey. That has to be a sign, right? Does it mean he wants us to get together and talk it out?

"There's Ricky," Melody says.

"I see him."

He and Sushil don't wait for the rest of us—they take off for the subway station.

"Should we follow them?" I ask.

"No. Gia, sweating him is not gonna help the situation. He's got to get over it in his own time," Melody says.

Xavier says, "Gia, if he doesn't want to be your boyfriend, I'm available."

He's grinning like he's just said the funniest thing ever. I give him a sad smile in return. "I'm not looking for a new boo, Xavier. But thank you for thinking of me."

Melody puts her arm around my back. "Let's just try

to have fun, Gia. We're gonna ride the bumper cars and the Cyclone. Then we're gonna go to the beach and scope out the hotties. Think about Ricky later!"

"Okay, I'm stoked now," I say.

"I don't hear any stoke in your voice, but I'm gonna ignore your grumbles. We will have fun today!"

It's a beautiful day—warm enough for the beach but not so hot that we'll want to hide inside all day. It takes us over an hour to get to Coney Island; all of us are crammed into multiple subway cars.

"Are you having fun yet?" Melody asks as we set out walking down Surf Avenue.

"Not yet, but I'm sure you're not gonna stop till I get enough."

Melody narrows her eyes. "That is a quote from somewhere, right?"

"Are you kidding me, Mel? Michael Jackson!"

"Oh, right. I thought it sounded familiar."

She gets the side-eye, lifted-eyebrow combination. How could she not know that?

Xavier says, "I feel like a mack! I've got two pretty ladies on my arm. Ladies, may I treat you to a Coney Island hootie dawg?"

You can't have a conversation with Xavier and not end up laughing. He reminds me of Adam Sandler with his crazy voices.

"I'll take a hootie dawg!" I say. "I'm hungry."

"I will not take a hootie dawg. Do you know that they put pig lips in hootie dawgs?"

Xavier laughs. "Then pig lips is mighty tasty!"

He goes into the restaurant while Melody and I wait

for him outside. I can't stop my eyes from darting back and forth over the groups of people, hoping for a glance of that Titans jersey.

"Relax, Gia."

"What? I'm cool!"

Melody chuckles. "You are the opposite of cool, girl. But I know you're trying, so I'm not going to trip."

"Taste this!" Xavier hands me a hot dog smothered in mustard and sauerkraut.

I close my eyes and take a bite. "Mmm! Thank you, Xavier."

"Let's walk over to the bumper cars," Melody says. "Y'all can eat those in line."

"Okay."

Between Xavier's clowning, Melody's pep talks, and hootie dawgs, I am actually having a good time. It's not enough to make me stop thinking about Ricky, but at least it's in the background of my thoughts.

We're standing in line for the Cyclone roller coaster when my phone buzzes. I almost drop it on the ground snatching it out of my purse.

"Calm down before you break it," Melody says.

"It's a text from Ricky!" I squeal.

Meet me on the boardwalk in an hour.

"He wants me to meet him on the boardwalk," I say.

"Is that all he said?" Xavier asks.

"Yes. Is that good or bad?"

Melody says, "I think it's good. He wouldn't ask you to meet with him if it wasn't something good."

"What if he wants to break it off for good?"

Melody asks, "Is that what you really feel deep down inside?"

"I don't know."

Xavier says, "As soon as we get off the roller coaster, we'll walk you over there."

"Shouldn't I go alone?"

"I think so," Melody says, "but we'll point you in the right direction."

I'm so nervous I can barely contain myself. I keep telling myself that this is Ricky, but it doesn't help. There are about a million butterflies in my stomach all flitting around at the same time.

Melody and Xavier walk me to the boardwalk entrance. I don't need them to take me all the way there, because I see Ricky standing there looking out at the water.

I walk toward him, first slowly, but then my steps quicken. Suddenly, I can't get to Ricky fast enough. I step up beside him.

"Ricky." My voice trembles, and I don't even try to hide it.

"Gia."

Ricky pulls me into a tight hug. Like he's never gonna let me go.

"Come on. Let's walk," Ricky says.

We walk in silence for a few moments. We're not holding hands, but we walk closely enough that our bodies touch.

"Gia, I need to ask you a question."

"Okay . . ."

"But before I ask it, I want you to know I won't ask it again."

"What's the question?"

"And if you say no, I don't think I can be friends with you at all. It would hurt too badly."

"W—what do you want to ask me?"

"Gia, will you be my girl?"

I want to yell out yes at the top of my lungs, but my voice is stuck in my throat.

"Say something, Gia. I can take it if the answer is no."

"No! No. My answer is yes! I want to be your girl-friend."

"You do?"

"Yes. Senior year, prom, Homecoming. I want to share all that with you too."

Ricky hugs me again, and this time when we separate, he leans in and puts a sweet, chocolate-flavored kiss on my lips. My head spins, my stomach churns, and my heart melts. Just like I thought it would!

"You know, I had a dream you took someone else to prom," I say to Ricky as we start to walk again, this time hand in hand.

Ricky shakes his head and laughs. "What? I've never wanted anyone else but you. Senior year is gonna rock."

Umm, yeah! It totally is!

COOL LIKE THAT

Nikki Carter

ABOUT THIS GUIDE

The following questions are intended to
enhance your group's reading of
COOL LIKE THAT.

Discussion Questions

1. Is Gia wrong for liking Rashad? Why or why not?

2. Have you ever been caught between two crushes? Did you pick one and ditch the other? Were someone's feelings hurt?

3. What did you think of Gia's adventures in New York City? What big city would you like to visit?

4. Should Gia and Melody have reported Sienna when she came into the dorm intoxicated? Would it have helped or hurt Sienna's situation?

5. Gia learns a lesson in forgiveness—namely, you have to forgive people if you want to be forgiven. Who have you forgiven lately? How did it make you feel?

Gia's Girl-Power Summer Playlist

Gia's got a soundtrack playing in her mind at all times! You can rock with Gia by listening to some of her favorite tracks.

Song	Artist
★ Porcelain Doll	Chrisette Michele
★ Single Ladies	Beyoncé
★ Trust	Keyshia Cole, featuring Monica
★ Turn Me Loose	Ledisi
★ Fear	Jazmine Sullivan
★ We Belong Together	Mariah Carey

A Discussion with the Author

1. **Coke or Pepsi?**
   Pepsi.

2. **What are your favorite TV shows?**
   Friday Night Lights, Smallville, Grey's Anatomy, and *Heroes.* (Save the cheerleader, save the world!!! Yeah!)

3. **Bath or shower?**
   Both.

4. **What's your most embarrassing moment?**
   I was at a house party in my good friend's basement. I went upstairs to get a snack and when I headed back downstairs, I slipped and fell down the flight of stairs. The music stopped, but I just hopped up and started dancing. Trust . . . it was ALL bad!

5. **Who's your favorite actress?**
   Sanaa Lathan! *Love & Basketball* is one of my favorite movies!

6. **Who's your favorite actor?**
   I have more than one. Johnny Depp, Denzel Washington, and Idris Elba!

7. **Who's your favorite singer?**
   This changes a lot. Right now I'm feeling Beyoncé, Alicia Keys, and Jennifer Hudson. I also like fun gospel artists like KiKi Sheard.

8. **Have you ever been in love?**
   Yes!

9. **If you could be a celeb for a day, who would you be?**
   Hmm . . . Kimora Lee! She is running thangs. So fabulous!

10. **Flip-flops or Crocs?**
    Umm . . . neither.

11. **What should readers learn from the So For Real series?**
    The lesson is that it's okay to be unique and fearless! You can be a Christian and fab. Also, the people who appreciate you for doing YOU are the ones you want in your life!

Want more?
Don't miss these other novels in Nikki Carter's
So For Real series.
Available now, wherever books are sold!

The telephone wakes me. Actually, my alarm clock *tried* to wake me, but I hit that snooze button four times.

"Talk to me," I say into the phone in my husky, man-sounding, morning voice.

My best friend, Ricardo, answers. "Gia, wake up. I know you're still in bed."

"How do you know?"

"Because you sound like James Earl Jones. You're going to miss your audition."

"Okay . . . I'm up. See you at school."

I throw my body out of my bed, my feet landing with a *thud*. I don't smell breakfast cooking, so that must mean my mother, Gwendolyn, is out with the street ministry team and I'm on my own.

I open my bedroom door, take two steps, and I'm standing in front of the refrigerator (yes . . . our duplex is that small). Gwendolyn has left me a note. It reads:

God morning, baby. I'm with the evangelism team. Eat some cereal and have a great day.

Why do I have the corniest mother on the planet? She says "God morning" instead of "*good* morning" because, and I quote, "This is the day that the Lord has made. I will rejoice and be glad in it." It's a wonderful scripture and a great thought by my mother, but nobody ever thinks it's funny—not even her friends on the evangelism team.

Gwen will go straight from street witnessing to her job as an LPN at Gramercy Hospital. An LPN is like one step below being a *real* nurse, but my mother couldn't afford to finish the rest of her college degree. She blames that on my deadbeat father, who hasn't paid a nickel in child support since I was a baby. I've only seen him a couple of times, actually, but I don't think it bothers me much. You can't miss what you never had, right?

I think about my audition and feel a little bubble of excitement in the pit of my stomach. My cousin Hope and I are trying out for the Hi-Steppers. It's a drill team/dance squad that is full of the most popular, prettiest, and desired girls in the school.

Hope is one of those popular, pretty, and desired girls. I am their polar opposite.

So why did I let Ricardo talk me into auditioning? Because we will be sixteen this year, and I'm tired of being lame. Don't get it twisted—I'm happy that I have straight A's and proud as I-don't-know-what to be in advanced placement classes, but my social life is the pits.

By the end of this year, my sophomore year, I want to

accomplish three things. First, I need to talk my mother into letting me get a relaxer for my hair. Second, I need to have a guy ask me out on a date, even if my mother doesn't let me go. It would be especially cool if that date was to the Homecoming dance. And third, I need to get a job, so that I can upgrade my entire social situation.

What am I going to wear? After one quick glance around the closet that I share with Gwendolyn, I see it's going to be the usual. A Tweety T-shirt and jeans. Today, I'm going with the red Tweety and faded blue jeans. Hope begged me to borrow one of her little Baby Phat couture outfits for the Hi-Stepper audition, but I refuse to walk up in that piece, sparkling and bedazzled. If they can't see past my faded jeans and Tweety T-shirt, then they are just not ready for me. Plus, Hope only offered her clothes because she's embarrassed of mine.

My cell phone is ringing again. I dash back into my room to answer it before it goes to voice mail.

"Talk to me."

"You really need to stop saying that. It's not cute."

I smile, because I know that my phone etiquette gets on Hope's nerves. I do not care. "Hey, Hope. What's crack-a-lacking?"

"Also not cute. Are you dressed?"

"Somewhat."

Hope sucks her teeth. "That means no. Have you even showered?"

I run down the hallway into the bathroom and start the water. "I will be ready in ten minutes."

"Sure you will. Me and Daddy will pick you up in twenty minutes. Do you want me to bring my flatiron?"

"Nope."

"Well, I'm bringing it anyway."

"I'm wearing a ponytail."

Hope sighs. "It better not be a nappy ponytail, and you better not be wearing one of those Tweety T-shirts."

"Okay! Bye."

I slick my dark pro style gel on the front of my ponytail, tie it down with a scarf and jump into the shower. The warm water feels good splashing my body. I close my eyes and imagine myself wearing that red and black Hi-Steppers uniform and the cute white boots with the tassels on the front. The thought makes me smile.

I can do this.

After my shower is done, on goes my jeans and on goes my boy Tweety. A lot of people think that Tweety is a girl, but he is a boy. Right now, Tweety is my boyfriend. Anyway, I don't care what Hope says, I'm wearing my shirt and I'm wearing my ponytail. I top off my whole look with a short jean jacket and gold hoop earrings.

It's a good look—well, as good as I can come up with on my limited budget.

The horn on my uncle's Benz tells me that it's time to go. I take one last look in the mirror, slick some baby hair (or baby hurrr if you're from the south) on my forehead, and give a little pat to my afro puff.

I'm not really mad at Hope for suggesting that I flat-iron my hair. It always looks great when I do, but my hair is long and thick and as soon as I take one step out the door and into the humidity—it's back to the giant curlfro. So, until I can break Gwendolyn down and convince her that a relaxer is very necessary, I'm rockin' rough and tough with my afro puff.

On the way out the door, I grab a snack-size bag of Doritos. Do Doritos count as cereal? They're made out of corn, so I'm thinking maybe.

I open the door, take a deep breath, and smile up at the sun. Even though it's September, it still feels like summer. All that will change in a month or so, because here in Cleveland we get snow in October.

"Gia! Quit soaking up the sun and come on!"

I squint angrily at Hope, who has her window rolled down and her shiny lips puckered. "I'm coming!"

I run down the raggedy walkway and, as usual, trip over a loose piece of gravel. I don't fall, but I do drop my book bag and spill out some of my folders. I don't know what it is, but lately, I've been super clumsy. It feels like I can trip over air sometimes. It's just something else about me that drives Hope crazy.

Hope gets out of the car to help me. She rolls her eyes at me and says, "Dang, Gia. If you can't even walk to the car, how do you think you're going to be a Hi-Stepper?"

"Whatever, Hope."

I roll my eyes right back at her, snatch my book bag, and get into the car. I could've said so much more than "Whatever." Like the fact that Hope has no rhythm and how she can't even snap her fingers and step at the same time, so how does she think *she* can be a Hi-Stepper? I'm gonna leave it alone, but she better not make me go there.

"Good morning, Gia," my uncle says.

"Hi, Pastor."

Okay, I see the question mark on your face, so let me explain. My uncle Robert is also my pastor. I never call him Uncle Robert, even though he's my favorite uncle. Everybody calls him Pastor Stokes or just Pastor, even my mom, and he's her little brother.

Hope gets back into the car too, and slams her door. "Gia, I thought I asked you not to wear one of those Tweety T-shirts."

Pastor Robert answers for me. "Hope, you are not the boss of Gia. She can wear whatever she wants."

Hope whines, "But, Daddy! She is going to embarrass me. We are trying out for the Hi-Steppers today and she comes out the house looking a mess."

I shout from the backseat, "I don't look a mess!"

"You're right. You don't look a mess—you look a *hot* mess," Hope hisses. "You did this on purpose."

"Whatever, Hope! You act like I'm thinking about you when I pick out my clothes. I'm just that into you, right?" I say sarcastically.

"You *are* that into me! Obviously. You only wanted to be a Hi-Stepper after you heard I was trying out. Why don't you get your own thing?"

"Hi-Stepping is not *your* thing. If you had a thing it wouldn't be Hi-Stepping! It would be looking in the mirror all day counting your pimples!"

Hope cries, "Daddy!"

I can't believe that Hope used to be my favorite cousin. We had "Best Friend" everything—bracelets, necklaces, earrings, folders, and purses. But something happened when we got to ninth grade at Longfellow High School. All of a sudden, she was ashamed to be seen with me because my mom couldn't afford to buy me Baby Phat and Juicy Couture.

The summer before we entered the ninth grade, Hope's mom, Elena, gave her a makeover. She took her to the salon and got her hair straightened and her eyebrows waxed. When my mother saw Hope's new look, all she said was, "She looks grown and fast. No daughter of mine is going to look like that."

I think the fact that I'm growing up scares my mom. She had me when she was seventeen, and she thinks that I might end up like her.

She's got me messed up.

Ain't no way in the world I want a baby or an STD. A sista like me is going to college, for real. You feel me? Plus, I see how hard my mom has it and I'm not trying to go through that too.

Besides, right now, I don't even exist to boys.

I keep wondering when puberty is going to start for me. Hope has been wearing a bra since we were in the sixth grade. I still don't need one, although I wear one on principle. I can't wear an undershirt in the tenth grade.

When we pull up in front of our school, Hope quickly dashes out of the car so that she doesn't have to walk into the audition with me. I fight back the tears that want to come, because there is no way I'm going to let her see how much she hurts me.

Pastor Robert turns around in his seat. "Don't worry, Niecey. I've always liked your T-shirt collection, and your hair is unique. Hope doesn't know everything."

"Thank you, Pastor. See you later, crocodile."

"Bye, alligator."

That's an ongoing joke between us. When I was little I couldn't get that "See you later, alligator, in a while, crocodile" saying right. I always said, "Bye, bye, alligator." My uncle is so cool, even though he is a pastor. He goes out of his way to be a father figure for me because my dad is not around.

As I walk over to the gymnasium, where the auditions are being held, I see my friend Ricardo waving at me. I wave back and smile. Ricardo being there (even though he's supposed to be at football practice) makes me feel so much better.

"Hey, Ricky. Does Coach Rogers know you're here?"

"Yeah, he said it was cool," Ricky replies. "Plus, I'm not starting this week anyway."

"Seriously? Why not?"

He shrugs his broad shoulders. "Some college scouts are coming to see Lance. He could get a scholarship."

Everybody, including Coach Rogers, knows that Ricky should be the starting quarterback for the Longfellow Spartans. But since he's only a sophomore, he doesn't get to play as often as he should. Their senior sensation, Lance Rogers, is the coach's son, so you already know what it is.

"What about the college scouts seeing you?"

Ricky says, "God is going to open a door for me, Gi-Gi. Don't worry about it. Right now, you need to get your head in the game and remember that step we came up with."

Ricardo's older brother, Jordan, is in college and in a fraternity. We used some moves from the Q-dog step show and hooked up a slammin' routine for my audition. Now, I just have to get it right.

Ricky and I walk confidently into the audition. He sits at the top of the bleachers with the other spectators, and I sit in the front row where the other future Hi-Steppers are waiting. Hope pretends to not see me come in.

Hope's friend, Valerie, who is captain of the Hi-Steppers, smiles at me. I smile back and try to make it not look super fake. I know she only pays me any attention because she likes Ricardo. A lot of the girls here are nice to me for that very same reason.

What they don't know is that Ricky would never holler at any of them. He's saved and wants to be a virgin when he gets married, after college. Some girls think that's weird for a guy, but not me. These little trifling girls are always writing notes about the nasty things they want to do to him, but he's not even on that. Plus, two years ago, when he had braces on his teeth, thick glasses instead of contacts, and more bumps on his face than a pizza has pepperoni, none of these girls even said hello. Especially not Valerie.

Hope is the first one up to audition. She hands Valerie a tape with her music on it and then walks to the center of the gym. Hope looks really scared, but she's smiling anyway.

The music starts and Hope does her little routine. It's obvious that Valerie helped her choreograph it because there are a few signature Hi-Stepper moves that Hope could never have thought of on her own. If she smiles any harder I think her face might crack and all her icy pink lip gloss will run down her shirt. Seriously, Hope looks like she tripped and fell lips first into a tub of Vaseline. She finishes and takes a bow, and all of her friends hug her as she comes to sit down.

I've got to admit that it was better than I'd expected. Much better. Hope might actually have the potential of being a decent Hi-Stepper. She gets on my nerves, but I gotta give props where props are due.

After a few really, really bad auditions, it's finally my turn. I give Valerie my tape and walk to the center of the gym with a cane in my hand. The cane was Ricky's idea.

The drumbeat of Destiny's Child's "Lose My Breath" blares from the speakers and I start my complicated routine. My stomps and claps are perfect, and everybody gets pumped when I tap my cane, toss it in the air and catch it with ease.

When I'm done, I get a standing ovation from the entire Hi-Steppers squad. Ricardo is also yelling and clapping like he's lost his mind. This is a good moment—the stuff of legends. Okay, maybe not legends, but it's really, really great!

Are bridesmaid dresses supposed to itch?

I'm asking because my mom, Gwen, has me standing in front of the church wearing a ridiculous amount of pink taffeta and some other material that's making me itch. I close one eye and try to concentrate on making the itch disappear, because it's in the center of my back, right where I can't reach it.

The concentration isn't working, so I shift my shoulders in little circles trying to reach the itch with the zipper on my dress.

"Gia, will you *stop* it?" hisses my cousin, Hope. "Auntie Gwen is gonna get you when she sees you squirming on her wedding video."

She's right. Gwen will be heated. But it's her own fault. She shouldn't have picked outfits that make us look like Destiny's Child backup dancers. All of this shining and glistening is a bit extra if you ask me. The only good thing about this dress is that it amps up my miniature curves. Yes, I have officially gone from skinny to slim. You don't know the difference? Well, boo to you. The distance from skinny to slim is about the same as the distance from thick to plump. Marinate on it.

Even though I'm sixteen and on my way into the eleventh grade, this is Gwen's first wedding. She met a guy at our church named Elder LeRon Ferguson and they really hit it off. Even the pastor (who is also my uncle) was happy about them getting together. On the real, I think the only two people *not* happy about this whole blessed affair are me and Elder LeRon's daughter, Candy.

Don't get it twisted, I want my mother to be happy, get a man and all that, but I just thought it would all take place after I was grown. I am so not in the mood for a new daddy and a bratty little sister who will probably make my life miserable.

But if Gwen is going to be upset 'cause I'm trying to scratch my itch, then she's gonna be extra heated when she sees Candy on video. She practically stomped down the aisle and didn't even hold her flower bouquet up in front of her. She let her arms drop to her sides and mean-mugged the video guy all the way to the front of the church.

This itch is really starting to drive me nuts. This whole wedding ceremony thing is taking forever, too! Gwen had to go all out and have three flower girls and a miniature bride. I mean, for real, is all that even necessary?

As the third flower girl marches up the aisle throwing flowers everywhere but on the floor in front of her, Hope leans forward and whispers, "There's Ricky."

We both smile at *my* best friend Ricardo. Umm . . .

yeah . . . survey says no. Hope needs to pause all of that action immediately. She's been lightweight digging Ricky ever since Homecoming of last year. And that's only because he got upgraded to "hot" status by Longfellow High's resident vixen, Valerie. She's the captain of the Hi-Steppers dance squad and not exactly my favorite person.

Ricky smiles back at us and waves. Even though I'm standing in the front of the church, I can tell he's looking real fresh and real clean. My mom would say he looks dapper in his church suit and tie. But I ain't Gwen, and *dapper* is a word for those old movies.

I know what you're thinking, and the answer is no! Ricky is just my friend, not my *boyfriend*. Gwen is dead set against me dating until I'm in college. This is not an exaggeration either. I totally wish I was exaggerating.

Finally, Gwen starts marching up the center aisle of the church. It's about time! When the entire congregation turns to watch her, I take my bouquet and try to scratch my back with the little plastic holder thingy.

My mom looks real pretty, kinda like me but older. She's grinning from ear to ear as everyone takes pictures of her. Since her only close male family member is her brother—my uncle, Pastor Stokes—she decided to walk down the aisle alone.

When I asked if Pastor was going to give her away, these were her exact words: "I'm a grown woman, and I belong to God. I'm giving myself away."

Oh the bluntness.

I am glad when Gwen makes her way up the three little steps to stand in front of Pastor and next to Elder LeRon. She looks real fly in her off-the-shoulder bridal gown that

Hope and I helped her pick out. Aunt Elena helped too, but she's my uncle's wife and Gwen isn't really feeling her all like that.

Pastor Stokes starts up with his standard wedding sermon. He's talking about love, forgiveness, and all kinds of stuff I don't need to worry about right now. My new stepsister, Candy, sighs loudly like she's bored out of her mind. But Gwen gives her some serious I-will-cut-you-if-you-mess-up-my-wedding-day side eye and she pulls herself together quickly.

After the vows are exchanged, and Elder LeRon kisses my mom, the ceremony ends, although we have to stand up here letting everyone in the church hug and kiss us. I am so not feeling that. I've got about fifty different shades of lipstick smeared on my face, and everyone's breath is not fresh. I mean, if you're gonna eat an onion and pickle sandwich you can at least respect the personal space perimeter or get yourself some extra-strength Altoids. For real.

Speaking of people who don't respect personal space, clammy-hands Kevin is standing in line with his grandparents. Kevin has been in love with me for like ever, and trust, it is completely against my will. And why did he just wink at me? Boy, bye!

"Here comes your boyfriend," teases Hope.

Candy overhears and scrunches up her nose. "That's your boyfriend? You have horrible taste."

"Kevin is not my boyfriend," I argue. "Hope is the one who went out on a date with him."

Hope pinches the back of my arm and frowns. She would love to forget her "date" with Kevin. It was really supposed to be my first date with Romeo, a football player at Longfellow High. But Hope was in straight hater mode and invited herself on my date. That's why she ended up chilling with Kevin for the evening. Let's just say that was not a fun outing for Hope.

Actually, though, even though Kevin is the opposite of everything fab, he is a whole lot better than Romeo. Months have gone by, but I'm still somewhat irritated about how Romeo played me. You don't just get over a boy taking you out on a date and leaving you stranded at the beach, just because you won't get freaky with him.

I know that Jesus would forgive him, but I'm still getting there, okay?

Kevin finally makes it through the line and hugs everyone, including me. "Gia, you look really pretty."

"Thank you, Kevin," I reply with a tight smile.

I almost said something smart, but I'm practicing accepting compliments graciously. And if I do say so myself, outside of this pink, frilly monstrosity, I do look kinda hot! My hair is especially fresh because Gwen gave me a two-stranded twist-out.

I see you giving me a blank stare, so let me explain. My mom washed my hair and then put cream and gel in and twisted it down my back until it dried. Then she untwisted it and let the waves hang down on one side and pinned it up in the back.

Yeah, reread that and take a mental picture. Just trust me, okay? It's fly.

Next in the line is Ricky. Hope reaches ahead of me and hugs *my* best friend. I think I need to keep saying that, because Hope doesn't seem to understand. She's trying my patience.

Then Ricky hugs me too. "Are we going skating after the reception?"

"You know it!" I reply and give my boy a high-five.

Hope frowns at me. "Do you think you could act like a lady for five minutes?"

I roll my eyes at Hope and ask Ricky, "Can you scratch my back?"

"Gia!" exclaims Hope.

Ricky and I crack up laughing because we know this irritates Hope. Hope and I have only recently renewed our BFF status. We went through some drama during our freshman and sophomore years, but we're cool now.

Even though we're friends again, we have very different ideas on what is fab and what isn't fab. Hope thinks that wearing designer clothes and making sure her lip gloss matches her purse is fly. The only matching I do is to make sure I have on two of the same socks. Outside of that, it's a free-for-all.

Finally, it's time to head over to the church social hall for the wedding reception. Gwen got Sister Benjamin, from the kitchen ministry at church, to cater, and I'm getting super hungry thinking about her fried chicken and sugar yams. I'm about to get my serious grub on.

Hope, Candy, and I sit at the wedding-party table waiting for our food to be brought by the servers. I'm in chill mode, but Candy is looking like a straight hater with her arms crossed and her face pulled into a haterific frown.

"What's wrong with you, Candy?" asks Hope.

Candy looks Hope up and down and says, "Mind ya' bidness."

"Ugh," replies Hope. "You would be cute if you weren't so evil."

"And you would be cute if . . . well, nah, that would never happen," says Candy.

Can I just say that I agree with Hope? Candy has long, thick hair that she wears in a braid down the back of her head. Her eyes are big and pretty too, and she's got smooth dark brown skin with not even one pimple.

But Hope is right. Candy is not just evil . . . she's super-duper evil.

I never thought I'd meet anyone as sarcastic as me, but Candy has got me beat for real. Anytime she opens her mouth an insult comes out of it. Even if you say something nice to her, she gives off nothing but negativity.

It's not a good look.

"I'm going skating with you," Candy says as if it's true.

"Um . . . no you're not," I reply.

She lets out an evil cackle. "Oh, yes I am. I already asked your mother and she said that you had to let me come."

What! We'll see about this. I march right on down to the other end of the table where the new Mrs. Ferguson is grinning and cheesing. Yeah, she can calm all of that down, because we need to have a conference.

I tap Gwen on the shoulder and she looks up. "Hi, sweetie. The food will be out in a minute."

"Okay, but did you tell Candy that she could go skating with me and Ricky?"

She pauses for a moment like she's trying to remember.

Then she says, "Yes, I think I did. LeRon and I think you two should get to know each other, since you'll be living under the same roof."

"Mom, that's not fair. She's not even nice, and I don't want her around my friends." I know I'm whining, but I really am not feeling this.

Gwen frowns. "Too bad. She's your new sister and sisters stick together."

"But, Mom!"

"Deal with it, Gia!" Gwen fusses. "Don't make me get ugly with you on my wedding day. You are about to make me mess up my makeup."

Elder LeRon sits down next to my mother and asks, "Is everything all right, Gwennie? Gia, why are you frowning?"

Gwen gives me a look that says, *You better not say anything.*

So, I don't. I go back down to our end of the table and eat my food in silence. Not even Sister Benjamin's extra crispy chicken and sugary yams are making me feel better. And Candy isn't helping either, sitting there with a smirk on her face.

Candy leans over and whispers, "I told you, Gia. Your mother wants me to like her and she's going to do anything I ask. Me and you are going to have lots of fun this year."

Why do I get the feeling that her idea of fun is my idea of torture?

The answer is *no ma'am*. Actually, the answer is a big, fat *no ma'am*. There is no way I'm going to say yes to this foolishness, no matter how much my mother, Gwen, begs. No matter how much my aunt Elena gives me that puppy-dog stare.

The answer is no and that's final.

What is the question, you ask? Well, Aunt Elena has a big idea. She calls it a big idea, and it's big all right. A big, fat hot mess. But since she's the pastor's wife everyone, including my mother, is going to back her up.

She wants to start purity classes at our church and she wants me to recruit girls to participate. And not just girls from our church, but girls at school too. Why doesn't she just ask me to make a sign that says LAME and stick it on my forehead?

Of course, I'm down for being a member of the purity class. Because the flyness that is Gia Stokes is also the purest of pure. But I don't have any plans to go around the school announcing my virginity! That would be social suicide.

So I'm sitting here on my mother's favorite couch with my arms folded and a fierce frown on my face, while Gwen and Elena try their best to tag-team me.

"Gia, you are a youth leader! The younger girls look up to you," Elena says.

"She's right, Gia," Gwen agrees. "You would be good at this."

"Did anyone ask Hope to do this?" I ask.

I pose this question because Hope is the obvious choice. It would make sense since she is the pastor's daughter. Shouldn't she be required to endure the embarrassment of being part of the pastor's immediate family? She certainly gets to enjoy the perks!

"I did ask Hope, but she didn't want to do it," Elena replies.

I look to my mother for help. "So, she gets to refuse, but I can't?"

Gwen says, "You neglected to mention that you asked Hope and she said no. I thought the two of them were going to work on this together."

Elena laughs. "You can't expect Hope to do something like this. She's not really cut out for it. It would come across better from Gia. She's more studious."

So my aunt is pretty much calling me a lame. And lames are supposed to be virgins, right? If I close my eyes tightly and concentrate really, really hard will I be able to stop time and escape this madness?

"Are there going to be any boys in the classes?" Gwen asks.

Aunt Elena laughs. "Of course not. This purity class will culminate in a debutante ball. I've never heard of a boy debutante."

"Well, boys should learn about purity too," my mother argues.

"That will have to be something for the men to address."

You've got to be kidding me! So, not only are we going to have a purity class (which I'm sure will be uncomfortably embarrassing), but they're going to parade us around in poofy white dresses to prove that we graduated.

Good grief.

How about we talk about the reason my aunt came up with this ridiculous idea to begin with? This all started when my cousin Hope decided that she was going to go stark raving boy crazy. Now Aunt Elena is all twisted, thinking that her precious daughter is going to become a teen pregnancy statistic or something. Hence, purity classes.

Hope pretty much flipped her wig at the beginning of the school year when she chose my best friend, Ricky, as her first big crush. She and Valerie, my co-captain on the Hi-Steppers dance squad, both competed for Ricky's affection. It was utterly ridiculous.

And holla! He didn't pick either of them. I think he actually picked me! I say that I *think* he picked me because we haven't worked out all of the details on that. But, on the night of the Homecoming dance, he gave me a Tweety charm bracelet.

And that was totally something.

Clearly it was something, because you don't just buy your best friend jewelry. Especially when that best friend is the perfect choice for a girlfriend! But it's been two weeks since Homecoming and there have been no can-I-be-your-boyfriend follow-up activities. Not a note, not a wink, nothing! Not even one of those distressed "I hate that I like you" looks like that teen vampire from *Twilight*.

Nada. Zilch.

Gwen says, "I think that both Gia and Hope should recruit girls for the purity class. Y'all need to start with that fast-tailed Valerie."

Can you tell that Gwen no likee Ms. Valerie? My mother has had beef with Valerie since she gave me a makeover when I was in the tenth grade. She also helped me sneak out on a date and other assorted foolishness. So, yeah, Gwen has her reasons.

I want to remind Gwen of what Jesus would do in this scenario, but I also want to continue breathing, so I decide against it.

"Mom, Valerie will not want to be in the purity class. Plus, I don't know if she qualifies. Do you have to be a virgin to be in it?"

Because if the answer is yes, Valerie is sooo not on the recruit list. I mean, I don't think she qualifies as an actual skank or anything, but she's pretty close. We're talking major non-virginal activities.

"Absolutely!" says Elena. "The whole point of the class is to encourage young ladies who haven't taken that step yet."

I almost laugh out loud. Unfortunately, I think Hope and I are gonna have a hard time finding anyone in the junior class that will qualify. Maybe we'll start with the freshmen.

"Okay, Aunt Elena. I'll pass out a few flyers, but I'm not making any promises."

Elena kisses my cheek. "Thank you, sweetie!"

"But only if Hope has to help!" I add.

"Oh, all right," Aunt Elena says. "I'll tell Hope that she needs to assist you."

Gwen says, "Candy will help, too. The three of you will make a great team."

I groan loudly. Candy is my all-around irritating stepsister. I spend enough of my downtime with her as it is, seeing that she macked her way onto the Hi-Steppers squad. Now I have to take purity classes with her, too! So not the bidness.

My phone buzzes at my hip, taking my attention away from Gwen and Elena.

I read the text message from Ricky. **Hey you!**

See, this is what I'm talking about. What exactly does *hey you* even mean? Is that a greeting for a home girl, or for someone you're trying to holla at? I think Ricky is purposely being ambiguous (go find your dictionary, boo) so that he doesn't have to deal with the possibility of *us*.

Since I don't know if I want to deal with that either, I understand his pain. But I'm going to need him to snap out of it and declare what the whole mystery of the Tweety bracelet means.

The Tweety bracelet that I've been rocking every day like my *boyfriend* gave it to me!

I text Ricky back with an equally ambiguous: ☺

Take that, Ricky Ricardo.

"Who are you texting?" Gwen asks.

Mmm . . . kay. Why is Gwen all up in my bidness?
"Ricky."

Gwen narrows her eyes and shares a glance with Aunt Elena. "Good grief. You girls are going to ruin Ricky with all of this attention."

"I agree. He's not the only boy on the planet," Elena adds.

"Uh, I'm only responding to a text that my friend sent me. You two are completely out of control."

Why is it that when I'm finally getting my little shine on, everybody wants to throw powder on it? Nobody, especially Aunt Elena, had any problem with Hope's desperate chasing of Ricky! Did anyone tell her to pump her brakes when she was writing him twenty-page letters?

The answer is no.

Did anyone tell Hope to stay home when Ricky made it abundantly clear that he was not trying to be her date for the Homecoming dance?

Yeah . . . that would be another *no.*

So they can absolutely save the hateration. They can save it for some time in the hopefully not-too-distant future, when Ricky is actually my boo.

Oooh, hold up a second. I'm going to have to give myself a lame citation for using the early 2000 term *my boo.* Womp, womp on me!

Gwen sighs and says, "We are not out of control. You young ladies are out of control, which is exactly why I'm one hundred percent for this purity class. All this boy chasing and carrying on must cease."

Did I just roll my eyes extra hard? Yeah, I totally did.

"I agree, Gwen. It's time we put our feet down and stop this madness!"

Okay, seriously, Auntie Elena is moving her mouth and sound is coming out, but she's not making one bit of sense.

"I said I'd be on your recruitment squad! Can I please be dismissed? You two don't need me in the room to discuss the state of today's teenager!"

Gwen narrows her eyes and turns to Elena. "Do you see what I have to deal with?"

"Hope isn't any better," Aunt Elena replies.

A growl escapes my lips as I storm off to my bedroom. I plop down on my brand-new Tweety comforter and pull my phone out. It's buzzing again.

Hi-Steppers meeting in two hours at IHOP.

This time it's Valerie blowing up my phone. I already know what she wants to meet about. The Longfellow Spartans are going to the state football championship, and we have to do an extra-special routine.

Valerie should be glad she's still on the squad after what she pulled at the Homecoming game. She was extra heated that she didn't win the Homecoming Queen title and take over the halftime show. She had the drum major in the marching band give a speech about her and everything.

It was bananas!

Somehow, I think Valerie still isn't over the loss to quiet little Susan Chiang. She blames every single last person on the rally girls spirit squad, my cousin Hope included, for not getting that Homecoming Queen crown.

And if she's not over it . . . then the war is not over.

If I was one of the rally girls, I'd be taking cover. They're going to be walking down the hallway, and out of no-where someone's going to yell "Man down!" just like Keyshia Cole's mama on that reality show.

And trust . . . it's going to be *all bad*.